WOLF

Charles Whiting
writing as
Leo Kessler

SAPERE
BOOKS

WOLF

Published by Sapere Books.

24 Trafalgar Road, Ilkley, LS29 8HH

saperebooks.com

ISBN: 978-0-85495-555-8

'Frankly, this English performance seems to me farcical: the latest reports of all these prohibitive regulations, these restrictive measures and so on. Normally that sort of thing isn't done when one plans an operation like this. It's all so unnecessary. They can assemble their forces there, embark them and ship them across to here and we can't find out what they're up to. I'm inclined to think that this is sheer impudent bluff!'

Adolf Hitler, 6 April, 1944

BOOK ONE: *THE INTERROGATION —*
TRENT PARK
(APRIL, 1944)

'Seventy-six days to go'

CHAPTER 1

'*Sechs Uhr, meine Herren!*' the duty NCO bellowed and slapped his hand against the canvas of their tent. '*Aufstehn!*' Then, as an afterthought, because after all they were both officers, he added a '*bitte*' before tramping off through the grass to the next tent.

Wolf woke at once, quietly and without fuss, save that, as always in these last four years, he glanced at his boots and his pistol hanging from the tent pole. They were both there. For a moment he stared up at the ivory glow of the canvas above him, knowing that this was the day and that he was committed; there was no way back now. Then he sprang out of his camp bed and slapped the pilot in the other bed across his blanketed rump, crying almost joyfully, 'Up!'

'Shit on you!' the pilot cursed and groaned.

Wolf grinned and, naked as he was, threw back the tent flap and went outside.

The spring sun sparkled on the dew, while, beyond, the Channel, ruffled a little by the wind, was being transformed from a dull green to light violet. Even to his untrained eye, it looked a perfect day for flying. He nodded his approval and, bending over the big tub of icy water, began to wash himself; it might well be a while before he would be able to wash again.

He was half way through his cold-water shave when the pilot, *Oberleutnant* Schmitz, stumbled out of the tent. Like Wolf, he was naked, but his body was flabby and he wore his fur-lined flying boots.

'Shit!' he grunted thickly and ran his right hand through his over-long blond hair, which was tousled badly because last night, in his drunken state, he had forgotten to wear his hairnet, 'Look at the weather. It's bloody perfect!'

Wolf flicked a piece of soap from beneath his right nostril and began to scrape away at his upper lip. 'You should be glad,' he said.

Schmitz gave him a sick look, as if he were out of his mind. 'With the Tommies out there and perfect visibility like this! I can see you're a typical field-grey. Know nothing about flying.' He trudged across to his tub of water, dipped one forefinger in it carefully, shuddered, and changed his mind about washing. Instead he moved across to the pile of red oxygen cylinders behind the tent, his open boots flapping clumsily, and began fumbling with one of the attached masks.

At that moment, a howling sound arose across the new emergency field, which grew to an ear-splitting crescendo. Wolf looked up. One of the reconnaissance squadron's Me 110 Es was beginning to bump its way across the field, trailing a cloud of dust behind it. He glanced at his watch. It was six ten. The Messerschmitt would be the first of the day to try to penetrate the thick screen of flak and fighters which the Tommies had built up along England's south coast since New Year's Day. More would follow every thirty minutes, until it was their turn at zero eight hundred. How many would come back was anyone's guess. Last month alone the Hermann Göring Reconnaissance Wing had lost ten planes trying to penetrate the English defences. Berlin had insisted that he should know such things, even down to the names of the missing pilots. He shrugged and wiped the last of the soap from his face. It was no concern of his. *He* wouldn't be coming back, at all events.

Behind the tent the pilot was taking deep breaths of oxygen, the mask clasped tightly to his face, as if his very life depended upon it. Wolf watched him and asked, after a while, 'What are you doing that for?'

The pilot dropped the mask, his face no longer so sickly looking, and stared at Wolf. 'I shall give you three reasons, *Herr Oberleutnant* whoever you are,' he answered with mock formality. 'One, the oxygen gets rid of an exceedingly shitty head, the result of too much calvados last night. Two, with what's going to be facing us soon over there, I need to cure the tremble in my hands rather smartly. Three, just before I came out into this freezing blizzard which the Frogs call spring, my eye chanced to fall on the thought for today on the calendar which my Aunt Klara sent me for Christmas.'

'And what was the thought for today?'

'"No one can say in the morning, what the evening will bring."'

Packed into the cockpit, encumbered with oxygen mask, parachute, and life belt, they rose slowly from Samer Field and began to fly south-east. At 3000 feet the pilot levelled out over Cap Gris Nez. He nudged Wolf and indicated their front. 'England two kilometres away.'

Wolf shaded his eyes against the glare from the perspex and stared at the white smudge of land.

'Dover,' Schmitz said, as if to anticipate his companion's question. 'Tommy's got his main radar station there. In a couple of minutes they'll have us on their screens — and then the trouble will start.'

Wolf nodded his understanding, but said nothing.

'As soon as we cross the coast, I'll come down to four hundred metres, flip the plane on its back and then you'll go for your little walk in space. On the back, you'll get out more easily. Clear?'

'Clear.' The pilot was right. In training he had jumped only from the old Junkers 52 and they were designed for parachuting. The Me 110 wasn't. The pilot's suggestion would prevent him from being injured leaving the plane.

'How far are you going in, Schmitz?'

'Just enough to give you a bit of terra firma under your feet; then I'm making dust. The Tommies will be on to us like a flight of vultures.'

The grey wall of exploding flak had just ended over Dover, and the smoke had begun to drift away, when Schmitz spotted them in his rear-view mirror.

'*Jesumariachristus*!' he cursed. 'Spitfires — three of them!'

Wolf struggled round. Three grey shapes, their wings painted with new white Invasion stripes, were flashing across the sky towards them, closing up at a tremendous speed.

'New clipped-wing Spitfires,' Schmitz said. 'Fifty kilometres an hour faster than this old crate!' He thrust the throttle right back and broke left.

Violet flares lit up the length of the attackers' wings. White and red tracer zipped by them and Wolf could hear the clack-clack of bullets striking the Messerschmitt. He glanced out of the cockpit. They had just passed the cliffs. They were over Kent. 'Roll her,' he yelled above the chatter of machine-gun fire.

'Now!' the pilot yelled back. He thrust the controls forward. The Messerschmitt started to go down in a series of tight spirals. Wolf felt his stomach rise unpleasantly. But the trick didn't throw off their attackers. They followed, machine guns chattering at eight hundred rounds a minute. The earth raced up to meet them. Red warning lights flickered on and off alarmingly. Below, the country revolved crazily. Suddenly she shuddered. Her motor backfired once, twice, three times. Wolf glanced at the pilot. The sweat was streaming down from beneath his leather helmet. Desperately he tried to level out. Wolf knew they were going to crash.

'Can't you do *anything*?' he screamed, thinking of all the planning which had gone into this flight.

'Yes,' *Oberleutnant* Schmitz cried. 'This.'

He touched a switch and the undercarriage went down. Behind them the Spitfires stopped firing immediately and the stricken plane, braked by the wheels, started to level out, while the pilot tugged frantically at the controls to bring her up. A moment later he had succeeded and, with her engine silent and the three Spitfires following at a respectful distance, the Messerschmitt started to glide towards the green fields of Kent.

'Why have they stopped firing?' Wolf cried.

'Because I put my undercarriage down.'

'So what?'

'That signifies that I'm shitting well surrendering.'

The earth raced towards the stricken plane, thick black smoke now pouring from its engine, a grove of trees, red roofs, a narrow winding gravel road; then they were over a village at a hundred metres.

'Cockpit!' Schmitz ordered, concentrating on the forced landing. Wolf reached up and, pulling off his oxygen mask, thrust it back. Cold air streamed in. The plane struck the earth and bounced up again in a thick cloud of dust. It hit the earth again. The undercarriage gave. There was the ear-splitting screech of rending metal as the plane tore across the field on its belly at the speed of a racing car. It narrowly missed a clump of oaks and seemed about to flip up on its battered nose when

Schmitz caught it, just in time. Wolf felt a hard tug as the safety belt dug into him and then the plane came to a halt at the edge of the field. For what seemed an age the two men remained strapped in their seats, enjoying the sensation of relief. Then Schmitz said, 'I knew we wouldn't do it. Come on; we've got to destroy this crate, or they won't give us our pensions after the war.'

Steadily the pilot set about destroying the plane before the Tommies came for them, while Wolf stood guard, his pistol drawn. The drill was simple. With his pocket knife Schmitz sawed through the petrol feed and allowed the petrol to flood into the ruined plane. Then he grabbed the roll of crepe toilet paper, which the Reich Air Ministry had prescribed for just such an emergency, and, dipping its end into the escaping petrol, began to unroll it.

They moved away from the plane; Wolf still held his pistol at the ready. He could already hear the sound of approaching motors.

Schmitz drew out the paper another ten metres before he was satisfied that they were far enough away from the plane. Then he lit a match and, cupping the flame with both hands, applied it carefully to the roll of paper.

Wolf had to do it — now or never. He clicked the safety-catch off. *Oberleutnant* Schmitz was saying, 'No one can say in the morning what the evening will...', when Wolf pressed the trigger. The side of the pilot's head exploded at the same instant as the leaking petrol caught fire.

CHAPTER 2

'Well, Squeak, I think it's about time we had him in,' Squadron Leader Taylor of RAF Intelligence said and puffed at his stinking briar which began to bubble. 'He's been in the cooler long enough to be ripe.'

'Yes, I think so now, Bubble,' answered Flight Lieutenant Tomm, otherwise known as 'Squeak' because of the noise his tin foot — a relic of the first 1,000 bomber raid on Cologne in '42 — made when he walked.

'London District Cage has had him for four days. He should be ready for our attentions.' He grinned at Taylor. 'Who's going to have him first?'

Bubble, who had gained his nickname from the noise his pipe made, thought for a moment. 'I think I will. Let's make this interrogation sweet and sour. I'll play sweet and you'll play sour. By now he's probably ready for a fag and a bit of sympathy.'

Tomm limped to the door which separated their two offices at the Trent Park, Cockfosters, HQ of RAF Intelligence. Squadron Leader Taylor picked up the official form on the prisoner and read it through carefully. '*Wolf... Oberleutnant der Luftwaffe... Aged 25 ... navigator in a Me 110 reconnaissance plane...*'

'Probably the Hermann Göring again,' he said to no one in particular. 'They've been coming in all last month and this.'

'*Shot down just off Dover... So far no statement about self ... see footnote.*'

Taylor glanced at the footnote. '*Pilot, Oberleutnant Schmitz, committed suicide just after helping to destroy the Messerschmitt.*'

Taylor puffed hard at his pipe. 'Strange,' he said, speaking aloud to himself. 'Why should the bugger shoot himself at this stage of the war? Strange — very strange.' He pressed the bell on his desk. Corporal Jackson, all stamping boots and brutal red face, popped his head round the door. 'Sir?' he barked at the top of his voice as if he were back at the RAF Training School.

'Send in the new boy, Corporal, please.'

'Sir!' Corporal Jackson stamped his right foot down hard and went out again.

The German navigator stood in the door. From behind the cover of his steel glasses, Taylor gave him a quick look. The German was tall and powerful-looking, with a bold face and the kind of quiet, tough eyes that Taylor remembered from good company commanders on the Somme in '17, who had somehow managed to survive the usual slaughter of subalterns and had learned how to become good soldiers. But he noted with surprise that, in spite of his appearance, the German only sported the ribbon of the Iron Cross, Third Class, and the Golden Sports Medal. What had he been doing these last five years?

'Please sit down,' he said in fluent German. 'All right, Corporal, you can go!'

'Sir!' Again Jackson stamped down his right foot.

Squadron Leader Taylor winced visibly at the noise and said, 'Are corporals as noisy in your Army too?'

Wolf said nothing. He was sizing the intelligence officer up. A base stallion, he decided, noting the faded medal ribbons on his tunic, called out of retirement or re-activated at the beginning of the war. There were plenty of his kind back in the Reich too.

Taylor pushed a box containing cigarettes towards him. 'Help yourself,' he said, smiling pleasantly. Wolf took the preferred cigarette and lit it. He took a greedy drag at the cigarette and felt his head swim. Taylor puffed stolidly at his pipe and said, 'All right?'

'Yes, thank you.' Wolf blinked his eyelids and told himself they weren't giving him dope. The von Werra Dossier had been categoric about that — the Tommies did not use drugs. It was just the effect of the strong American tobacco, the first he had tasted since 1939.

Taylor took his pipe out of his lips and said, almost apologetically, 'Well, I suppose we'd better get on with it. Now you are with the *Luftwaffe*, aren't you?' Wolf looked at him unbelievingly. What a stupid question when he was dressed in the *Luftwaffe's* blue-grey. His initial tension vanished. The man was obviously a fool. He began to relax.

The interrogation — if that was what it could be called — droned on and on. After a clumsy, half-hearted attempt to trick him into revealing what his mission over South-East England had been, Taylor seemed to forget military matters altogether. For a while he chatted about pre-war Germany, asking questions about the Hitler Youth, Strength-through-joy, the Nuremburg Party Days, so that Wolf began to believe that he was — or had been — one of those secret admirers of Hitler Maggie had told him about. Then Taylor went on to the causes of the war and why Germany had attacked Poland.

Dutifully Wolf played his role, while Taylor listened attentively, sucking at his pipe. The Versailles Diktat — the new German minorities abroad — the loss of Germany's colonies. He heard himself talking and was bored with the sound of his own voice. But Taylor seemed to find it all very fascinating and kept nodding his head, almost as if he were in agreement with his prisoner. Finally, however, he appeared to recollect where they were. He pulled out a battered nickel watch and said in English. 'Tut tut, almost time for lunch.'

Wolf kept talking until Taylor said in German, 'I'm afraid we must break off now, Herr Wolf. The spirit's willing, but the flesh is weak, you know.' He chuckled. 'One must eat, even in Intelligence.'

Wolf rose to go.

'Oh, just one question, Herr Wolf!'

'Yes?'

'Why did your pilot, Oberleutnant Schmitz, shoot himself?'

For a moment Wolf was caught off guard. This was the sting in the tail that the von Werra Dossier had said was typical of the British form of interrogation. The best reaction was to play it as cool and as off-hand as possible.

'We have a German proverb, Squadron Leader,' he said slowly. 'Money lost, nothing lost. Honour lost, much lost. But courage lost —'

'Everything lost,' Taylor completed the proverb for him, saying the words as if to himself. The next moment he had pressed the bell and the escort was stamping in once more to take him back to the cells.

'Well, Bubble?' Tomm asked as they took their places at the table in the mess. Taylor looked down at the shabby cloth. 'Not much, Squeak. Not much.'

Over the weak wartime beer, Taylor summed up his thoughts on Wolf for Tomm's benefit. 'There are a couple of things, I can't quite work out about him. One: we know the Hermann Göring has been trying to penetrate the beachhead areas ever since Christmas now — and has suffered pretty heavily in the attempt. But, why, at this late stage, use the most obvious approach, over one of the most heavily defended areas? Two: our man is twenty-six, according to his own statement; but have you seen his gongs? They are virtually non-existent. And you know how the Jerries love to hang bits of brass on themselves?'

'So where's he been and what has he been doing all the war?'

'Exactly. But it's point three which worries me most. Why did the pilot commit suicide?'

'*Mut verloren, alles verloren*', the German had said. Did that explain it? He had lost his courage too after Ilse's death, for she had been his '*alles*' after George. But he had kept on going.

'So what are we going to do about it? Sour this afternoon?'

'No, this evening, or perhaps later. Let him savour the sweet for a little longer and think we're fools. The sour will be more effective that way.'

CHAPTER 3

The skinny man in a vest, blue-grey *Luftwaffe* trousers and open flying boots was washing a pair of socks in the sink when Corporal Jackson pushed Wolf into the cell and slammed the door behind him. The man turned and Wolf saw that his face was a dull yellow; he looked Chinese save for the eyes which were round and occidental. He saw Wolf's surprised look and grinned.

'Yes, I know what I look like. When I bailed out, I pulled the marker fluid on the dinghy by mistake as I hit the drink. The result is this — dyed yellow.'

Wiping one wet hand, he thrust it out at Wolf, still holding the soapy sock in the other. '*Hartmann, Oberleutnant, Jagdflieger.*'

Wolf took the hand of the fighter pilot and grinned.

'Wolf, Navigator,' he said. 'Glad to meet you.'

Hartmann remembered the sock and dropped it into the sink. 'I'll do it later. Nice to have a bit of company in this place. You been upstairs?'

Wolf nodded.

'Which one did you have — the one with the pipe or the one with the tin foot?'

'The one with the pipe.'

Hartmann grinned, his teeth surprisingly white against his yellow skin. 'He's not bad — for a Tommy. What's he want from you?'

'What do you mean?'

By way of an answer, Hartmann held his finger against his lips. He mouthed the word 'bug' and indicated that Wolf should follow him to the window. He thrust it open. It was barred on the outside, but they could lean out a good half metre, out of reach of whatever listening devices the Tommies had placed in the cell.

'You can't be too careful,' Hartmann whispered, as they stood there, heads outside. 'You never know. I was shot down a week ago and they've been at me ever since.'

'Why?'

'They think I know something about the fighter defence of the new ski sites.'

'The what?'

'We've got them all over Northern France. *Reichsgeheim-sache* of course. They look like ski slopes from the air.

We're going to start firing the first of our new revenge weapons from them before they begin their Invasion. That'll make the Tommies crap in their caps.' The little yellow-faced fighter pilot paused and then said, 'So, what's with you, Wolf?'

Wolf opened his mouth and then closed it again more slowly. He had been four days in solitary confinement at the London Cage and it was good to speak to someone again. Yet he remembered the von Werra Dossier. How did he know that Hartmann was not a Tommy spy?

He shrugged carelessly. 'God knows! Last month they bagged most of my squadron but I'm nobody and know nothing important.'

Hartmann didn't appear to be listening. Instead his hand was feeling the edge of the window with anxious fingers. 'Just checking, you know. The Tommies might be smart enough to figure we'd open the window. Perhaps it was something you did before you joined your squadron?'

'I don't think so,' Wolf answered as casually as he could, walking back to his bunk. 'I think I'll get my head down for a bit. It's been a long morning.' And with that he closed his eyes and feigned sleep. Half an hour later the corporal with the red face fetched Hartmann for another session with the interrogators.

'No go, sir.' Corporal Rosenbloom said, grinning all over his yellow face, which he had to dye every second morning. 'He's a hard-nosed bastard. He knows the ropes. They must be briefing them better these days.'

'All right, Corporal, you did your best. Thank you.' Rosenbloom saluted and went out.

Taylor grinned. 'All right, Squeak. Now he's yours.' Now the 'sour' part of the interrogation could begin.

'Right, Jackson, wheel in the victim now, will you?' Tomm said, slipping into a Wing Commander's jacket which he always used on these occasions and placing a big Malacca cane on the desk.

Jackson turned at the door and bellowed in bad German, 'Inside, you Nazi swine!'

As Wolf went past, he elbowed him hard in the ribs.

'Thank you, Corporal,' Tomm said in English. 'I won't need you now. I don't want any witnesses, in case we have a little accident in here.' Jackson went out.

Tomm took his time, while Wolf noted the big black stick and the lamp, still unlit, but turned in his direction. He knew he was in for a rough time.

The Wing Commander rose and limped across to the blackout curtains. He pulled them to and switched on the desk light so that it shone directly on Wolf's face. 'My name's Tomm,' he barked. 'T-O-M-M, got it? So you can put me on trial as a war criminal if you win the war, which you won't.' He lifted the stick and brought it down hard on the desk in front of him.

'Now I want you to get this straight, Wolf. I hate Germans. I hate them from the bottom of my heart. They shot a big lump off me over Cologne Cathedral two years ago and I've never forgiven them for making me a cripple.' He leaned across the desk and glared at Wolf, his face crimson with artificial rage, pearls of sweat gleaming in his thick eyebrows. 'I eat Germans for breakfast. Get that?'

Wolf had known men like the Wing Commander in Russia. They had suffered so much that all they knew was how to hate. Nothing motivated them any more but hatred, and hatred was a much more powerful driving force than love. 'Then you had better have good teeth, Mr Wing Commander,' he said.

Tomm glared at him. 'Now I'm not going to mess about with you, Wolf. I'm going to ask you some straightforward, simple questions — and I want some straightforward, simple answers. *Klar*?' He slapped the cane across the desk again. 'Now, I know all about your damned Hermann Göring. We've got more of your pilots in the bag than you've got running around free on the other side of the drink. We know their names, their jobs. We even know what their girlfriends did for them in bed — those of your pals who were interested in girls, that is. So I'm not going to waste my time on that sort of refuse. I want to know this. What was your mission and where have you been all the war?'

'You have all the details I am allowed to reveal to you according to the terms of the Geneva Convention,' Wolf said coldly.

'You mean you have the audacity to say you are not going to answer my questions?' Tomm asked with mock incredulity, playing the role he had played over these last two years to the hilt.

Wolf remained silent. The von Werra Dossier had said that the Tommies never used force. But things might have changed since 1941. He tensed his body for the first blow. But Tomm didn't hit him. Instead he picked up the black stick and began thrusting it nervously through a ring formed by his thumb and forefinger. When he spoke again, his voice was less strident, more reasonable. 'Now, look here, Wolf,' he said, 'I don't want to have to start the heavy stuff. But you must realize I've got a senior officer on my back too, breathing down my neck, demanding results. Why don't you just let me have the answers I want? Who will ever know among your comrades or back in the Homeland? Besides what difference will it make?' He stopped his to and fro movement of the stick. 'We have girls for chaps who co-operate. All nice and discreet, with drinks and a comfortable room.' He slid the stick slowly through the tight circle of flesh. 'It's going to be a very long time in the camp without — well, you know.' He licked his lips. 'Now why don't you tell me what I want to…'

At that moment Wolf rose to his feet and, steeling himself, did what they had told him at the final briefing he must do. He hit Flight Lieutenant Tomm squarely on the point of his chin.

CHAPTER 4

'And then the cheeky bugger planted one right on me,' Tomm said incredulously and touched his jaw tenderly.

The Wing Commander in charge of Intelligence shared Taylor's grin for a moment. 'What do you think made him get so aggressive? It's most unusual.' He turned to Taylor. 'Can you ever remember a Hun socking one of our chaps, Bubble?'

Taylor shook his head.

Tomm shrugged. 'God only knows why he did it. Bonkers perhaps. They all go a bit funny for a few days after you get them in the bag. But this is going too far.' He grinned. 'You should have seen old Jackson's face! I thought he was going to blow a gasket when he saw me sprawled in the wastepaper basket with my arse in the air.'

The Wing Commander frowned. 'Now, listen. You know that the Air Ministry had designated the V-1 sites and Colonel Wachtel's Flak Regiment 155 as our number one priority.'

Taylor and Tomm nodded. RAF Intelligence had been looking for Wachtel and his regiment since February when he and his officers had last been spotted by the French Resistance in Paris. Since then they had disappeared and it was vital to find out what had happened to them; for Flak Regiment 155 would be the one which would launch the coming V-1 offensive against England, as soon as the Invasion started.

'So, I can't let you two lark around, wasting your time with this Wolf chap.'

'I know,' said Taylor. 'But I have a feeling about this one, that somehow he's special.'

'Oh, come off it. When you've been in this business for any length of time, you begin to suspect everything and everybody.'

'Yes, you're right, but somehow…'

'All right, I'll give you another forty-eight hours with him and if he hasn't spilled his guts by then, he's off to the naughty boys' camp.'

Eric Taylor had had his first serious dealings with the Germans after the Third Battle of Ypres when he had been left on the battlefield for dead and a German medical orderly, who could have been his father, had kicked him in the ribs to check whether he were alive or not. Thereupon he had groaned and a passing German doctor had kicked the orderly up his backside and called him, in the phrase of the time, 'a miserable pig-dog'. They were the first words of German he ever learned. At Holzminden he had learnt a good deal more, absorbing the language easily with the quick receptiveness of an 18-year-old. Six months later his knowledge of German had got him as far as the Dutch border and across at Venlo, where a fat Dutch border-policeman to whom he had appealed for help had sold him back to the Germans for twenty marks.

He remained in Holzminden until the end of the war when he went up to Oxford where he gained a First. His thesis had followed — a lucky choice of subject-matter for his first publication by Blackie's — an edited version of Goethe's *Campagne in Frankreich, 1792*. Surprisingly enough no one had ever thought of 'doing' the only one of the Master's works never previously published in England. For him it had been a kind of sentimental journey, back in 1923, tracing Goethe's steps through the ill-fated Prusso-Austrian campaign against the French in 1792 which had ended with the '*Cannonade at*

Valmy. The book established him as a minor figure in the field of German studies in England.

Thereafter there had been Heidelberg — the Neckar, the *Philosphenweg*, the ruined castle — and all the rest of that beautiful university town in the golden years of the Weimar Republic. He had met Ilse there — a student in one of his own English classes, the deadly boring *Phonetik II* — and taken her back to his first English academic post, assistant lecturer (temp) in German, University College, Hull. That same year, 1925, George had been born.

'How terribly English George sounds!' she had said in the ward, with the yelling bundle cradled in her thin arms. 'Then you will call him *Georg*,' he told her in German, 'and I shall call him George.'

Promotion and transfers had followed. Manchester, Leicester, a six-month sabbatical in Heidelberg, which he had not liked one bit. Now most of the students wore black or brown uniforms and there were brawls with the '*sozis*' and the few remaining '*Roten*' in the student pubs at night. He had been glad to return to England, although he had not managed to finish his commentary on Herder's *Journal meiner Reise*. In 1938 he had been offered, and accepted, the new Brotherton Chair in German at Leeds. That year Leeds swarmed with Germans, mostly Jewish refugees, but others also — Socialists and Communists. They weren't liked. At night the drunks would shout at the scared, pale-faced passengers on the trams heading for Chapeltown or Roundhay, where most of the foreigners lived; 'Get off back to Palestine or Germany, or wherever yer sodding came from!'

Ilse didn't like it, or the treatment in the shops when she opened her mouth and that trilled German 'r', which he had never managed to cure in *Phonetik II*, revealed her as one of 'them bloody Jerry Yids!' But she stuck it out, hanging ever more closely to Eric and to George, who was now a sturdy 14-year-old.

When, that Sunday, Chamberlain announced wearily that Britain was at war with her native country, she had wept a little, said a prayer for her two brothers, who would now be returning to the Army as reserve officers, and on Monday had gone to Moortown Police Station to register as an 'enemy alien'. (She had never applied for naturalisation — the two of them had not thought it important to do so.)

The long winter passed in bored inactivity. *Der Sitzkrieg,* 'the sitting war' ended in May, 1940. All of a sudden the Germans were attacking everywhere — Holland, Belgium, Luxemburg, France. Defeat after defeat. In the morning when he took the tram up the steep incline to the university, he would pass the recruiting office, with its confident posters of sturdy, broad-chested soldiers, sailors and airmen outside and that old appeal — 'For King and Country'. But he did nothing. Instead he talked of Herder's influence on Goethe to students who were becoming increasingly less interested.

Then, in that blazing hot June of 1940 his whole cosy, safe world had been destroyed. A lone Heinkel III, failing to find its target, dropped its bombs on a field just outside the Leed's suburb of Moortown and fled before the approaching Hurricanes. The bombs killed two boys searching the overgrown ditches for abandoned metal for the local scrap metal drive.

One of the boys was George.

On the day after the funeral, Ilse committed suicide. At the inquest the family doctor said she must have been hoarding sleeping pills.

Almost at once Eric had requested leave-of-absence, knowing, as he explained his reasons to an understanding Vice-Chancellor, that he would never go back to Leeds, or even teaching. At the onset of middle-age, when he thought he had solved most of life's problems, he realized he would have to begin again.

He had gone to the Army recruiting office, eager to submerge himself in the great unthinking mass of khaki, and the sergeant had turned him down flat. The RAF had been different. It was not every day that they had a university professor walking through their doors.

Thus he had come to RAF Intelligence. At first he had thought the technique of cross-examination was not much different from that he had used with his own students at a *viva*; one asked certain questions, based on one's own knowledge of the subject, and one received the answers one was searching for in due course. But, by 1941, after nearly a year at the job, he knew there was more to interrogation than that. Every prisoner was different and had to be played according to his temperament. Some could be intimidated by the loud voice, the heavy gestures, the knowledge that there was another man standing behind their back. Others were natural talkers, ready to tell you their life story at the drop of a hat, who could easily be guided in the right direction. Then there were some who would trade what they knew for favours.

There were a few, very few, who had already overcome the hopelessness, the despair, the lethargy, which afflicts all prisoners immediately after capture, who were already fighting back, giving as good as they got, challenging the interrogator the whole way, making him pay for every little bit of information.

Now, after four years of interrogation, he knew that such men could be divided into two categories: those who fought back, not because they knew anything important, but because they were bloody-minded; and those who really knew something the knowledge of which frightened them more than their interrogator.

As the one-time Professor finished his pipe and eyed the bottle of ration whisky on his bedside table, debating with himself whether he could afford a nightcap he wondered to which of the two types the new German belonged. And three floors below him, lying on his hard bunk, with the light burning into his eyes, listening to the simulated screams and blows which he knew were part of the softening-up process, *Oberleutnant* Wolf stared at the dirty, flaked ceiling of his cell.

CHAPTER 5

It was a simple ceremony. Wolf and his escort met the cortege party at the gate to the little churchyard. Schmitz's coffin, surmounted by a *Luftwaffe* cap and his Iron Cross, Black Wound Medal and the Narvik Medal placed carefully on the swastika flag, lay on a plain board cart, drawn by a skinny horse. It was just after dawn and the birds were singing in the trees that surrounded the suburban churchyard.

Taylor nodded and they stepped forward and lifted the coffin from the cart. It was surprisingly heavy. Slowly they advanced down the path, followed by a squad of RAF policemen, doing the slow march.

The Padre was waiting for them at the open grave. He was old and benign, with snow-white hair which matched his surplice. He saw Wolf's uniform and gave him a brief, shy smile as they put the coffin down. Then he began his brief sermon, reading from a small black book. 'Lord let me know mine end and the number of my days: that I may be certified how long I have to live...'

He had a beautiful voice, Wolf thought, only half understanding the words.

They lowered the coffin into the ground. The Padre sprinkled earth into the hole. 'Earth to earth, ashes to ashes, dust to dust...' the Padre read from his black book.

A sergeant barked a command. The RAF policemen stood, their feet apart, Lee Enfield's raised. The first volley of blank rang out. In the tall trees at the edge of the little churchyard the crows rose, squawking in protest. Twice, three times, drowning the slow mournful notes of the bugler, then the funeral was over. *Oberleutnant* Schmitz, well-known in *Luftwaffe* brothels from Berlin to Boulogne, was safely below ground. Wolf looked at Taylor expectantly, waiting for the order to move back to the vehicle which had brought them there. But just then the Padre crooked a slow finger at him and said in rusty, yet tolerable, German, 'I would like to have a word with you, my boy, before they take you back.'

Together, they crunched slowly down the gravel path, while from behind them came the sound of the gravediggers already beginning to toss earth on the coffin. When they were out of earshot of the others the Padre placed his hand on Wolf's shoulder and said: 'My son, you are going to be facing a difficult time in the months to come. To be a prisoner in enemy hands, when one is so young and the spirit and flesh are hot, is very difficult.' He tapped the line of faded medal ribbons on his white surplice for an instant. 'I know, for I was once a prisoner myself.' He gave Wolf that sad smile of his once again.

Wolf said nothing.

'You will undoubtedly know moments of despair. I did myself then and I was already a man of God. But you know, my son, we all have our spiritual resources which will get us over our despair, if we know how to apply them.'

'How do you mean, *Herr Pfarrer*?'

'In the camp — and undoubtedly they will send you to a camp soon — we must start afresh. We must clear our mind of the past and what we were once. We must extinguish it. Now in your particular case — and I see you for the first time this morning and know nothing of you — I feel you have something to hide. There is something from the past which is burdening you — something which you must get rid of *now*, if you are to survive the camp. Trust me, my son, I am a man of

God. Your secret will be safe with me, as safe as it would be with your own padre.' He looked directly at Wolf, exuding benignity, his ancient face framed by that halo of white hair, like that of a saint. 'What is it?'

It was then that Wolf realized the sheer cunning of the Tommies' charade this morning. 'I shall be relieved to tell you, *Herr Pfarrer*, and get it off my conscience.'

'Yes,' the Padre said, leaning forward.

'Well, it's like this — I don't like girls. It's the boys, you see!'

He laughed at the sudden, very unbenign look on the Padre's face, and Pilot Officer Jones, formerly of the Old Vic and Gaumont British Studios, said in English, in his normal hoarse cockney, '*Bollocks!*'

Just after lunch that day Jackson opened the door of Wolf's cell and sprang stiffly to attention. After a suitably dramatic pause, a young RAF officer entered the cell. He was very English-looking, the bright ribbon of the DFC on his chest and the tunic unbuttoned at the top in the way that young British fighter pilots affected. But his accent, in spite of his attempt to anglicize it, was pure Berlin. 'I say, sorry to burst in on you like this, but I'm the chap who shot you down last week.'

Wolf rose to his feet and took the proffered hand.

'Thought I'd look you up and say hello. Bit of practice for the old German too. Haven't used it much since Eton.' He dropped three packets of Senior Service on the bed casually. 'Brought you a few cigarettes. I guessed you would be out. Is that the way you say it in German?' He smiled winningly at Wolf. This was exactly the way the von Werra Dossier had described the Tommy approach back in '41. He nodded and said nothing, wondering what particular trick this one was going to try and pull on him.

'Haven't much time, old chap,' the fighter pilot went on. 'Can I sit on your bed?'

'*Bitte!*'

The fighter pilot sat down. 'Your pilot put up a pretty good effort with that old crate,' he said. 'Surprised you chaps are still using them — especially in a danger spot like Dover. Surely you must have known what it's like up there? Or did you get lost?' He chuckled awkwardly. 'You were the navigator? It was your pigeon, eh?'

Wolf saw the trap at once. 'I'm sorry,' he said. 'I am not allowed to talk about flying.'

The fighter pilot looked shocked. 'I say, do you really think I'm trying to pump you? Good God, I haven't sunk to that level yet. Just came by for a bit of a chinwag, that's all. I mean, I'm aircrew like you, just trying to see it from the other chap's point-of-view.'

'Old chap,' Wolf said, rising to his feet, knowing that there was worse in store for him than this and not wishing to expand his resources on a Berlin Jew who would fool no one, 'I think you'd better go.'

The fighter pilot rose to his feet too. 'Well, of course, if that's the way you feel about it.'

'I do.'

The fighter pilot left.

It was a long afternoon and an even longer night. Jackson, silent for a change, blacked out his cell early, and he was alone in the two metre square stone tomb, with even the obscenities washed from the walls during the time he had been outside at the 'funeral'. He was convinced that the coffin had not contained Lt Schmitz, but a heap of stones — hence it's unexpected weight.

Five-thirty passed. No Jackson with the usual 'tea' of cocoa and two thick slices of bread and jam. Eight o'clock, no supper either. At nine he thought he heard the thin wail of sirens, although he knew the *Luftwaffe* had not managed to bomb London for over six months. Time crept by. At a quarter past nine the cell began to shake alarmingly. There was the sharp crack of what he took to be flak and the thick crump of exploding bombs nearby. Heavy boots ran down the corridor outside, as if in alarm. Fists began to hammer at cell doors and he could hear faint voices in German, cursing and pleading not to be left behind. There was the harsh squeak of a rusty door being opened and an English voice crying, 'Come on, mate, make it snappy. *The ruddy place is on fire!*' Then someone ran up the corridor.

After that there was no sound, save the crash of the guns and the thump of explosives in the distance. He seemed to be alone. Wolf's eyes shot to the floor. A ruddy light had appeared at the crack below the door and the cell was getting perceptibly warmer. The bastards had forgotten about him. For a moment he panicked. They were going to leave him behind — to be burned to death! Already he could feel the heat filling the cell, and his body breaking out into a thick sweat. He sprang to the door, his fists clenched, as he prepared to hammer on the door for assistance. Then, just as suddenly as he had jumped up, he realized what they were up to. He relaxed his hands, and walking with controlled slowness to the radiator, touched it very gingerly. It was burning hot.

When Taylor came to fetch him for the first interrogation of that long night, he found him squatting on his bunk, his naked body lathered in sweat, a wet towel round his head and grinning, rather 'like Ghandi giving the British Raj a bit of the old-come-uppance', as Squadron Leader Taylor confessed to Tomm over breakfast the following morning.

They worked on the German all that day. During the course of their interrogations they carefully fed him as much tea as possible. Lunch was salty fried fish, very salty. When he thrust out the little flag (worked from inside the cell), indicating he wanted to go to the latrine, no guard came. His bladder was threatening to burst with all the tea and a whole carafe of water he had drunk after the fish. He hammered on the door. He knew what they were trying to do to him. They were trying to humiliate him into talking.

After a while, Jackson came. 'What do you want?' he asked from the other side of the door.

'*Pissen — ich will pissen!*' Wolf cried.

'*Latrine — besetzt,*' Jackson said in his crude German. '*Nix pissen, jetzt.*' He stamped away, laughing.

When his bladder could stand it no longer, Wolf took off his right flying boot and urinated into it. He limped into the afternoon round of interrogations with one boot on.

At four o'clock that afternoon, just when Tomm, hoarse, worn and irritated beyond all measure, was about to strike him with the heavy Malacca cane, he dismissed Wolf and called in Taylor, who had been listening at the other door. 'Strewth,' he croaked, 'I nearly did for the bugger just then!'

Tomm's red-rimmed eyes and the heap of cigarette ends in the ashtray in front of the Flight Lieutenant were eloquent testimony to the state of Tomm's nerves.

'He's getting you down, Squeak,' Taylor said.

'Of course the sod's getting me down.' Tomm caught himself just in time. 'Sorry,' he said, his voice under control again. 'I'm for giving up on him. I don't care if he knows that the Führer's grandma is a white-haired Jewess living in Whitechapel at this very moment, I'm giving him up. He's just too bloody-minded.'

Three hours later Taylor gave up himself, his voice as cracked and hoarse as Squeak's, his pipe bubbling furiously. As Jackson, an unholy light in his eyes, escorted a pale but unshaken Wolf out of the door for the last time, he unscrewed his fountain pen and signed the order transferring the prisoner to Number Three, the camp for the 'naughty boys', as the Wingco called it. It was the place they always sent such types.

'All right, hard-case, on yer sodding feet!' Jackson said as he opened the cell door.

Wolf stared up from his bunk at the red-faced Corporal and, behind him, two other RAF policemen, peaked caps hiding their eyes. '*Was?*' he asked, exhausted after the long day of interrogation. '*Was ist?*'

'Get him, mates!'

The other two policemen rushed forward. One grabbed Wolf by the hair and hoisted him to his feet, while the second man twisted his arms behind his back. Jackson thrust his face close to Wolf's and he could smell the stale beer on the Corporal's breath.

'Thought you was gonna soddingly well get away with it, did yer, yer Jerry bastard!' he snarled, pulling a single leather glove over the knuckleduster which he had already thrust on his right hand. 'Well, yer've got another think coming. Yer can do without them stupid officer sods upstairs, but not with yours

36

truly!' He nodded to the other two and they tightened their grip on the helpless German.

Next moment, Jackson's right fist crashed into Wolf's stomach. He gasped with pain, and the policeman's big hand clamped over his mouth, deadening his yell just in time. Jackson grinned, pleased with the effect of his first punch. 'Don't worry, mate. Nobody's gonna hear you in this place — and there's plenty more where that came from.' He slammed another vicious right into Wolf's ribs and the German sensed a sharp, stabbing pain in his ribs, as if one of them might have been broken.

'Fell getting out of the truck on the way to the Naughty Boys Home and probably hurt yer side,' Jackson sneered, and hit him again.

In spite of the pain, Wolf's heart leapt. Instinctively he knew that the officers had nothing to do with this. They were finished with him; Jackson was doing this for his own perverted pleasure. Then, when it seemed the beating would never end, Jackson gasped, 'Hold him right tight, mates. This is it!'

The other two grasped him even more firmly. An instant later, Jackson stepped back and, with all his strength, rammed his knee right between his legs. His scream of agony was stifled in the policeman's hand and then they let him fall, writhing and whimpering with pain on the floor. Yet, as he twisted and turned, he felt an overwhelming sense of triumph in his heart. He had done it. He had outwitted them. He was on his way to Number Three Camp.

BOOK TWO: *THE BRIEFING — NUMBER TEN PRINZ-ALBRECHT-STRASSE (FEBRUARY, 1944)*

'One hundred and twenty-five days to go.'

CHAPTER 1

The camouflaged Volkswagen jeep, which had driven them to Berlin from the Hunting Commando's HQ, stopped in front of Number Ten. Skorzeny, impressively enormous, got out first, stamped his feet on the pavement, and, nodding at Wolf, marched up the steps, still littered with rubble from the bombing raid on the night before.

The two helmeted sentries' eyes nearly popped out of their heads when they recognized the scar faced Colonel who had snatched Mussolini, the Italian Dictator, from his mountain prison the year before. Their white-gloved hands slapped their rifles audibly, as they came to the present, and their heads moved rigidly inwards, as if they were worked by steel springs. Skorzeny saluted in his casual Viennese way and held the door of the Reich Main Security Office open for Wolf to enter. '*Danke, Obersturm!*' Wolf snapped and smiled to himself. His chief would never learn how to act like a real German soldier; he was too much of an Austrian. An officer in the Wehrmacht, especially in the Armed SS, did not hold the door for his subordinates.

'*Nichts zu danken, lieber Wolf,*' Skorzeny answered, smiling all over his broad, scarred face, which looked as if it were the work of a butcher's apprentice who had gone mad with a carving knife. They passed inside and after showing their passes — a mere formality, since Skorzeny was known to every German — they were escorted to the second floor where SS *Brigadeführer* Schellenberg, the head of the *Ausland SD* and the newly assimilated *Abwehr*, had his office.

A red light was burning outside the leather-padded door and Skorzeny said, a little scornfully, 'Schellenberg is playing his tricks again. You'd think that this was a public cross-roads!'

Wolf smiled; He had heard of General Schellenberg's little tricks. The office was full of electrical gadgets. His desk was reputed to contain two twin machine guns which he could operate from a foot button in the unlikely event that anyone should penetrate far enough into the Reich Main Security Office and try to assassinate him. There was also supposed to be a sheet of bulletproof glass that came down from the ceiling in front of his desk and an automatic steel grating that came out and barred the door from inside at the touch of a button.

'He is just like Heydrich was,' Skorzeny was saying. 'Always reading those cheap novels about the British Secret Service.' Then the red light changed to green and the door opened automatically.

They went in. Schellenberg was waiting for them behind the big desk, as elegant, sleek and cunning as ever. He rose immediately, responded perfunctorily to Skorzeny's *Heil Hitler*, and after Wolf had been introduced to him by his CO, seized the young SS officer's hand in his own with feigned warmth. Wolf prevented himself from shuddering just in time. The Secret Service Chief's hand was warm, soft and somehow a little feminine.

He looked up at Wolf and said, as if he were honoured that the young frontline officer had found time to visit his new chief, 'It is very good of you to come, Wolf.' He extended a well-manicured hand towards the leather armchairs in the corner *Sitzecke*.

As they crossed to the chairs, he moved to his desk and pressed a button. The centre of the occasional table opened up to reveal a small bar, complete with glasses. 'You'll find anything you need there, but I wouldn't touch the whisky if I were you. It's not the real thing. Our friends across the Channel have been avoiding contact with us of late.' He beamed at them, obviously pleased with the gadget.

Schellenberg waited until Skorzeny had poured himself a cognac and Wolf had lit a cigarette; then he pressed another button. Behind him a panel slid away to reveal a huge wall map of Northern Europe from Norway right down to the Spanish border and including the British Isles.

'Your initial briefing, and remember, please, that it is a capital offence to reveal anything said in this room to a third party,' Schellenberg said. '*Verstanden?*'

'*Verstanden, Brigadeführer!*'

'Excellent. Now as everyone who reads the papers knows, Field Marshal Rundstedt in France, will, with the onset of spring, be daily anticipating hordes of gum chewing *Amis* and knobbly-kneed Tommies to be landing somewhere on that coast. They have been preparing for the business since 1942 and, slow as the Anglo-Americans are, they must be ready soon. Besides, if they don't come soon, the Ivans will be on the Channel coast before them and that drunken plutocrat Churchill would never allow the Russians to do that.'

Skorzeny and Wolf nodded their understanding.

'Now the major problem that has been facing my own organization and that of Admiral Canaris all winter has been exactly *where* they would land.' He pressed another button and a bright arrow of light flashed onto the map. 'You see the Reich has nearly five thousand kilometres of coast to defend. From here in Norway,' he directed the arrow to the north, 'right down through Holland, Belgium' — the arrow of light followed the coast by remote control — 'down through France to the Spanish border. Naturally our experts, for what they are worth, have narrowed down the possible area of attack to a five hundred kilometre stretch between Flushing, here,' the arrow stopped at the Dutch port — 'to Cherbourg, there. They base their conclusion on the fact that this is the only sector which can be adequately covered by British-based fighters. Clear, gentlemen?'

'Clear,' the officers answered in unison.

'Our experts conclude, further, that, within this five-hundred-kilometre stretch, due to the need for port facilities, the right kind of beaches for assault and re-supply, the potential points of attack can be limited to two areas. Here, at the Pas de Calais between Dunkirk and the mouth of the Somme, and here, in Western Normandy between Caen and the Cotentin Peninsula.' He beamed at them suddenly. 'And now the fun really starts, gentlemen. There are seriously varying schools of thought on where the enemy will attack. Rundstedt and the General Staff feel it will be the Pas de Calais. The main launching sites for the V-1 weapons are there and it would provide the quickest route to the Rhine and the Ruhr. The Führer, on the other hand, is not quite so sure. His well-known intuition —' He said the word without any change in facial expression, but to Wolf his voice conveyed exactly what he thought of the Führer's well-known intuition — 'has led him to believe that the enemy will attack in area two — Normandy.' He cleared his throat and continued. 'To complicate matters further, Marshal Rommel, who will be in charge of the actual ground defence, has formed an appreciation, which falls half-way between the other two views. He anticipates a strong landing at the mouth of the Somme, as does Rundstedt, but, well aware of the value in the past of the Führer's well-known intuition, he has come to the conclusion that there will be a strong diversion in Western Normandy.'

Schellenberg pressed another button. The map of Northern Europe disappeared to be replaced by a large, detailed map of England. 'England,' he said somewhat unnecessarily, 'where, undoubtedly, at this moment there are men such as us, planning the downfall of the Reich and the elimination of war criminals — such as us.' He chuckled at the thought. 'It would be amusing, my dear Skorzeny, wouldn't it to know exactly what they had on us?'

'Not for me, it wouldn't,' Skorzeny snorted, and buried his scarred face in his cognac glass.

'Now I have been told that from Calais on a good day, with the aid of binoculars, you can read the time on a clock in Dover,' continued Schellenberg. 'After all, England at its nearest point is only thirty-two kilometres away from us. Having said that, gentlemen, I must confess as head of the *SD* and *Abwehr* that we know as much about what is going on in England this winter as we do of the moon.' He paused and let his words sink in.

'Such agents as Admiral Canaris is purported still to have there are producing virtually nothing of importance. Radio traffic with them is almost dead because of the Tommies' security precautions. Now the Tommies have just gone one further. With effect from the first of February, all civilian traffic between England and Eire has been stopped, so we can't get information out that way. Nor through the Spanish diplomatic bag. It is regularly being searched by their Secret Service. And to cap it all, a coastal belt, fifteen kilometres deep, has been imposed from the Wash to Land's End.' The arrow of light traced the area on the map. 'And on either side of the Firth of Forth. Thus, if those poor excuses for agents which Canaris employs in England were so inclined to find out what was going on in the coastal areas, they would be stopped at the fifteen kilometre limit.'

Wolf was puzzled. 'I don't understand, *Brigadeführer*,' he said. 'We know the Tommies are going to invade us somewhere in France. Of what use would it be for our agents to attempt to penetrate the coastal belt?'

'If we could ascertain that the massing of the enemy invasion forces was taking place west or east of, say, Portsmouth, we could judge which area of France they were going to invade,' Schellenberg replied.

'Of course!'

'Yes, as simple as that. Then all the doubts and uncertainties would have an end. The Anglo-Americans have only sufficient strength for one main effort, say, in the region of a fifty-division attack. The amount of shipping needed to carry more would be beyond even their capacity. Of course, they will be trying subterfuge. They are past masters at it, especially the Tommies. But a trained eye at, say, Portsmouth or Plymouth or Dover would soon decide which was the chaff and which was the wheat.' He looked at Wolf directly.

'Aerial reconnaissance?' Wolf asked, trying to avoid that look and what it signified.

Schellenberg dismissed the *Luftwaffe* with a contemptuous wave of his hand. 'Fat Hermann,' — he meant Göring, head of the *Luftwaffe* — 'has let us down consistently since 1941. No one has any faith in him and his flyboys any more.'

'A raid by the Hunting Commando,' Skorzeny said suddenly, looking up from his glass, 'is out of the question. We could get neither a transport plane nor an assault boat across the Channel. They have it too well tied up.'

'How does one find out, then, the answer to that very simple question?' he asked, knowing as he asked it that he was

44

challenging fate and, in a way, not caring, for he had been challenging fate for a long time now.

Schellenberg pressed his fingers together. 'If,' he said slowly, 'we cannot do it from the outside, then we must do it from within. *You*, my dear Wolf…'

After Wolf had gone, Schellenberg waited till Skorzeny had finished his third cognac before asking laconically, 'Well?'

'A loner, Schellenberg. But an exceedingly good man and a volunteer, and we don't have many of that kind these days. We think very highly of him in the Hunting Commando — intelligent, aggressive, loyal and very tough.'

Schellenberg smiled. 'Exactly the type we require,' he said cynically. 'Bold, skilled cannon fodder.'

CHAPTER 2

Wolf ate his midday meal at the Officers' Home — *Eintopf mit Einlage* — ogled the pretty 18-year-old blonde who served it, and then, going to his narrow cell-like room, dropped on his bunk and began to think.

He was going back to England! England, after all these years, and Maggie! No, there would be no Maggie, whom he had once called Mother and whom he had loved — and still loved — more than he had anyone else in all his life. For Maggie was now the enemy.

Maggie was the only one who had really loved him, understood him, made him feel that he had belonged, in a world where he had never belonged; Maggie had always understood. Maggie was not the enemy, come what may!

In 1918, Wolf's father had accompanied the Kaiser into exile at Doorn in Holland. In that terrible year, several things happened which deeply affected Wolf's life: the Kaiser abdicated; the General — Wolf's father — decided that he wasn't going to go back to a Germany ruled by 'those buggers who had stabbed us at the front in the back' (though his own particular service at the front had been limited to four weeks in the summer of 1914 with his Uhlans); Wolf's mother died of Spanish Flu; and the General took Maggie Sibley, one of the maids at Doorn, as his mistress.

Maggie's father had been a Yorkshire shipper, settled in Rotterdam. He had been a medium-sized exporter of Dutch cheese, winter tomatoes and the like, to the North of England. When he died of a heart attack, Maggie had been left penniless and without a hope of being repatriated. Thus she had become a maid, moving from one job to another, as servants or master took a fancy to her strong, heavy-breasted body, until in 1918 she had arrived at Doorn, a 25-year-old virgin, with a passionate hatred of the Dutch, and an equally passionate desire to find out what all the fuss was about.

The General — Wolf's father — had satisfied her curiosity. More, he had quietly removed her from the Kaiser's household and established her in his own cottage, granted him by the crazy German consort of the ugliest and richest Queen in Europe.

The liaison — strange as it must have seemed to the surviving blue-blooded members of the Kaiser's court — thrived. Or, at least, it did until one day, the General read in the *Vossische Zeitung* of an attempt to take over Munich by an unknown ex-Army Corporal named Hittler or Heidler or something like that, and asked leave from the Kaiser to return to Germany and help destroy the weak, and obviously ineffectual Weimar Republic. The Kaiser refused.

This resulted in *General der Kavallerie* Hans-Georg Maria Wolf (*im Generalstab*) taking to *oude genever* and going the same way as Maggie's father within the year. They buried him in the small churchyard at Doorn on New Year's Day, 1924. On that same evening, Maggie and Wolfie (as she called him) were on their way to Harwich ferry, thanks to the 2,000 guilders which the General had gained on the speculative Amsterdam *Beurs* of 1920/1921.

They found him — his father's sisters, Frau Grafin Klara von und zu Brahmsee, gebornen Wolf and Fraulein Kornelia Wolf — one Friday teatime in the summer of 1930. He was sitting at the table, covered with a clean copy of the *Bridlington Free Press*, with *William the Detective* propped up against a bottle of sauce, eating his sausage and fried bread while he read, when there was a knock at the back door. Later he realized why it was the back door.

'You go, Wolfie,' Maggie called out from the front room where she was serving a similar tea to her 'guests'. 'Bed and all meals, including evening dinner, thirty shillings', the sign outside the seaside boarding house she had bought with the money she had taken from the General's safe, read. 'Be a good luv!'

And as he was always a 'good luv' for Maggie, he left his half-eaten sausage and went to open the back door. Three men were standing there. One he knew, PC Jenkins, the little resort's only policeman. The other two were strangers to him, but when one of them, who wore a monocle and spats, said to him, *'Ach, du bist bestimmt der junge Wolf, nicht wahr?'* he knew instinctively and with the overwhelming realization of a vision that his days with his darling Maggie were over.

Thus he came to the country in which he had been conceived but never yet seen (the monocled gentleman from the Embassy in London had said — through his solicitor, the other gentleman — that there would be no proceedings against Maggie on account of the money if she let Wolf go without a fuss) and was delivered into the hands of the hard-faced sisters.

The Wolf sisters existed in a rundown *Gründerzeit* villa on the fringes of Wiesbaden on the pension the Gräfin received for her husband, who had 'fallen' (as they always phrased it) 'before Verdun'. Food was tight, as well as love. Three times a year the two sisters put on the medals of the dead husband and the dead father and ate well — the Kaiser's Birthday, the Anniversary of the Victory over the French at Sedan in 1870, and, for some reason known only to themselves, 'Dead Sunday' in November, dedicated to those who had died in the recent war. Three times a year the growing boy ate himself sick and for the remaining 362 days hated the sisters like poison.

Twice he tried to run away, back to Maggie, who wrote to him in her ungrammatical English every week, but he didn't get far. The sisters were always quicker. In 1935, after Maggie had written to him that 'a lot of people seem to like your Hitler here on account of the fact he's against the Bolshies', he joined the Hitler Youth. In spite of his funny German accent, he soon became a Leader. But after a while he tired of the absurdity of the marches with the same old songs, the long lectures on the Führer — 'born under the most humble circumstances in Braunau-am-Inn' — and the systematic brutalization of the younger boys. He dropped out quietly — to the sisters' relief — and turned his attention to girls. And he was remarkably successful for a 17-year-old. But they only sufficed to assuage his loneliness, his feeling of being an outsider, for a while, and so he forgot girls and concentrated on passing his *Abitur* which he would need if he were ever to become an Army officer, the only career, according to the sisters, conceivable for a Wolf.

In June, 1937, he passed the high school examination and, a month later, he returned one afternoon with a grin on his face to tell the sisters that he had been accepted for the Armed Forces.

'Not the Fourth, your father's old regiment?' the Gräfin asked rapturously.

He shook his head.

'The Seventh?' Kornelia queried.

Again he shook his head.

'Which then?' they cried together.

'The Bodyguard!'

'The SS!' they exclaimed in horrified unison. 'Not the SS — oh, the shame of it!'

Two weeks later he left Wiesbaden for the training school at Bad Toelz and neither saw nor heard of the Wolf sisters again.

Maggie's letters continued to follow him wherever he was posted until he received her final one, dated Sunday 3 Sept, 1939, which said that she thought 'I'd better not write any more. But I still love you, Luv. Maggie.' He had been handed it on his way out of the military hospital — the wound he had received in Poland had been more complicated than the bone menders had first thought — on his way to join his Regiment, which was already massing for the attack on Holland.

But that May there was no time to think of Maggie or anything else but war and death. The months, the years passed. Holland, France, Yugoslavia, Greece — one desperate action after another. The cauldron of Russia which destroyed the Bodyguard — it was now a division — time and time again and in which only the veterans, the cunning, able, lone-wolf veterans like himself, survived, hardly learning the names of their new subordinates before they were swallowed by the ever-greedy maws of war.

In the summer of 1943, he had been ordered to take a relief company of panzer grenadiers to take over a section of the front outside Belgorod in Central Russia, held by *Hauptsturm* Sanders' Company. But when he and his men had crawled the last fifty metres to a strangely silent company area, they found that there was not a single man of the Sanders Company left. They had died where they had fought, the Russians piled up in earth-brown heaps in front of their slit trenches.

He found Sanders' command post. Sanders was dead, a bullet neatly drilled through the centre of his forehead, but erect and on his knees, his hand on the pin of his last grenade. Behind him his *Rottenführer* was dead too, head bent over his Spandau. All around there were dead SS troopers, not one of them over 18, their weapons still in their lifeless hands, untroubled by the flies crawling over their waxen faces.

Mechanically Wolf had waved the flies away from Sanders' face, realizing as he did so that Sanders was the last officer in the whole of the Bodyguard who had marched with him against Poland in September, 1939. He was alone again!

Two weeks later he volunteered to join *Obersturmbannführer* Otto Skorzeny's mysterious *Jagdkommando*.

Thus it happened that Wolf lay on his bed in the Berlin Officers' Home that February afternoon, thinking of the past and realizing, as always, that he belonged nowhere and to nobody, save perhaps to Maggie, if she were still alive; that he would never love or be loved; that he was a loner, condemned to be one until he was dead.

As the sirens started their thin wail again, signifying the return of the Tommies, he said aloud to the ceiling, 'The Lone Wolf, eh?' and grinned.

Five minutes later he was washed and dressed. Ten minutes after that, he had bought two bottles of black market champagne from a frightened Air Force corporal outside the *Lehrter Bahnhof*, while the crowds of shabby, scared civilians streamed to the station's shelters. An hour passed and he had convinced the pretty blonde Red Cross assistant to share the 'champus' with him in the gloom at the back of the Officers' Home shelter, to celebrate his 'departure for the front'. One and a half bottles of champagne later, she had seen the urgent necessity of sacrificing her virginity to this handsome young man, who was obviously on his way to a certain death.

CHAPTER 3

'I would like to tell you a little story, my dear young friend,' Schellenberg said to Wolf the next morning, as if he were incredibly old, instead of a well-preserved 37. 'One evening last week, a group of German officers in uniform with the red flashes of the artillery clearly visible on their epaulettes for any lurking enemy agent to see, left the *Gare de Lyon* in Paris in a number of taxis, driven by my own men. Undoubtedly they were seen and their directions to the drivers to take them to our Headquarters in the *Avenue Kléber* clearly heard by the French Resistance agents who were expecting them at the station.' He smiled. 'They were meant to be.' He paused for dramatic effect. 'Now those officers did not reach that address in the *Avenue Kléber*, as the French agents who regularly watch our HQ there will by now have undoubtedly reported to their masters in London. They disappeared during the journey.' He smiled at Wolf, as if he expected him to make some comment. But Wolf remained silent.

'So,' Schellenberg continued, his voice a little more hurried, 'what had happened to those German officers of the artillery? I shall tell you. During the course of that journey across Paris, they changed into a varied collection of disreputable French rags and disappeared into the streets of the capital, indistinguishable from those all around them.'

'Why?' Wolf asked.

'Those officers belonged to Colonel Wachtel's 155 *Flak regiment*. Now you may ask what is so important about a flak regiment that it goes to such lengths to disguise its movements. Indeed when I last heard from him, Colonel Wachtel himself had actually gone to the length of beginning to grow a beard, absolutely contrary to Army Regulations, eh?'

'Certainly, *Brigadeführer*,' Wolf agreed.

'But, you see, Wachtel's Regiment is not an ordinary artillery formation. It is a specialized unit which will fire our V-1s against the enemy when the Invasion begins.'

'But, *Brigadeführer*,' Wolf objected, 'you said yourself yesterday in the initial briefing that the Tommies know where the V-1 sites are. That is why Field Marshal von Rundstedt thinks the enemy will attack through their location in the *Pas de Calais*. Why then all the mumbo-jumbo and the attempts at concealment?'

'Oh, for God's sake tell him,' Skorzeny grunted angrily and helped himself to his first cognac of the day.

'The sites are there, my dear Wolf, and the Anglo-Americans have known their whereabouts since last year; hence their many attempts to destroy them, fortunately without too much success. But, since we first invented the V-1 and the British learned of its invention through traitors and spies, we have pushed research much further and come up with this.' He pressed a button on his desk. On the wall behind him, there appeared a long grey-looking object, with what seemed to be an exhaust above its tail, mounted on a heavy truck.

'What you are looking at,' Schellenberg explained, 'is the second stage of the V-1. We have motorized it! And that is where Wachtel and his officers have disappeared to. They are training the officers and men of a new flak regiment. We have given it the cover name of 50 *Sturmpionierregiment*, to account for the trucks and heavy equipment — which is completely mobile and can be moved to any part of the front in a comparatively short period of time. With sixty trucks at their disposal and a firing time of one V-1 per hour, they could concentrate their fire on any invasion beach and drop sixty tons of high explosive on it every sixty minutes. Do you understand what that would mean to the enemy's chances of successfully carrying an assault across an open beach?'

Wolf did. 'It would mean that firing from a range of ten kilometres, they could wipe out the enemy assault in one devastating salvo and be on their way to another location before enemy air could locate them.'

'Correct. The existence of the *50 Sturmpionierregiment* could change the whole character of our defence of France.'

'But I don't see what this has to do with me and the location of the Anglo-American invasion forces in England, *Brigadeführer*? Why do you need me?'

Schellenberg hesitated, feeling an inner glow of triumph. The young hero, eager for an early death, had bought the tremendous pie. Skorzeny buried his nose in his glass, as if he were embarrassed.

'Because of this,' Schellenberg continued. 'There is only one catch in the 50th's mobility — the stockpiles of V-1s needed to feed them. In the *Pas de Calais*, we have already seen that the RAF, unable to knock out the sites, have gone after their stockpiles, which we had spread over Belgium and Northern France. The Resistance betrays the sites to the Tommies all the time. But why should they begin looking for such sites in the Normandy area if they do not know of the existence of the 50th? There are, therefore, two reasons why we must find out where the enemy invasion force is being concentrated,' Schellenberg went on, knowing now that he had the SS officer convinced — the man was leaning forward in his chair, tense with repressed excitement. 'One, to be able to conceal those missiles efficiently in time somewhere near the Normandy beaches. Two, to be able to convince the High Command and, perhaps, the Führer, who knows just how limited the supply of V-1s coming from the factories is, that they must be located far from the *Pas de Calais* area, where, as you know, Rundstedt expects the invasion to come. Now it is a risk that cannot be taken. We cannot have, say, half our missile stockpile out of reach of the *Pas de Calais*. But if we knew for certain where the invasion was coming — south or north — then we could hide the 50th's missiles with an easy heart and know that on the day the Anglo-Americans came streaming from their assault boats, we would wipe them off the face of France with impunity.'

Schellenberg had lingered over his tea, as if he wished to give the young man time to back out. But Wolf had said nothing, so when the white-jacketed SS orderly had cleared away the tea things, he began the final stage of his briefing. Operation Cuckoo's Egg, as he called it to himself, could start.

'Let me state this, categorically, right from the outset, Wolf. No one has escaped from an English PoW camp since von Werra in 1941 — I shall give you his dossier at the end of this briefing — and in the end he was only able to return to the Reich via Canada. Understand this, once we have parachuted you into England, there is no way back for you from there till after our victory and the Anglo-American surrender.'

'I understand, *Brigadeführer*,' Wolf said.

'Excellent. But I had to warn you. Now we have one agent in place in Southern England whom we still trust. In addition, he still possesses an *AFU*, a secret radio transmitter, which he has been ordered to use only in the most dire emergency. He will be the man who will transmit your information when you have it. Again, I shall give you his details at the end of this briefing?

Wolf refrained from asking why the agent in question could not carry out the assignment himself. He was too taken up by the mission for that. Besides at the back of his mind a little voice was saying softly, but insistently, there was one sure place he could run to, once he had regained his freedom in England.

'Now it is essential that after your capture you are sent to Number Three Prisoner of War Camp, located at Stockbridge — here.' A button was pressed and another. The big map of Southern England appeared on the wall, as if by magic, and the arrow of light pointed to an area between the coast and Andover. 'Number Three is the only German PoW Camp still in existence in the whole of that part of England — the rest were moved last year when the Allies started to move up their pre-invasion forces. Why, you might ask…'

'Yes,' Wolf interrupted him, 'I can see its location is excellent for our purpose, but not for theirs. It's too close to the fifteen kilometre prohibited zone.'

'Agreed. But you see Number Three is a special camp. Its inmates are those of our forces who will not be broken by the British — pilots, officers of the U-boat Service, comrades of yours from the Armed SS. They are all hard men, who have committed some supposed war crime, refused to take part in democratic indoctrination.' Schellenberg said the phrase as if it were in quotes. 'In short, they are difficult, dangerous men, who are to be kept in an area where the Allies' frontline troops are to be found, where they can be discouraged from attempting to escape right from the start because all around them there are thousands of military establishments, manned by the best soldiers the Allies have.'

'I understand, *Brigadeführer*,' Wolf said. 'But if that is the case, how would I be able to escape from camp Number Three in the first place.'

'Because,' Skorzeny broke his long silence, 'we have a plan.'

Schellenberg smiled and sat back in the big leather chair.

His subordinate had come in right on cue; he was playing his part in the great deception, although Schellenberg knew that, in his heart, Skorzeny did not like it. 'A plan, which we hope will throw the whole of that part of England in a turmoil and allow you to accomplish your mission before you are recaptured by the British.'

There was no sound in the big office after Skorzeny had finished save the metallic tick of the wall clock and the sound of someone sweeping away broken glass and rubble in the courtyard below.

'Well?' Schellenberg said finally.

Wolf nodded slowly. 'It will be difficult,' he said. 'Those men will have to trust me one hundred per cent before they will follow me on such a venture.'

'They will, Wolf. You will make them.'

'How?' Wolf asked bluntly.

'By giving them back a purpose — a belief that they are not simply vegetables, useless creatures who cannot possibly have any influence on the war any more. You must make them believe they can still do something. They are desperate men. With the right leader, they will be prepared to carry out a desperate venture, even if it costs them their lives. After all, it is for the sake of the Reich — its very existence,' he added, tongue in cheek.

Wolf was not fooled. He knew Schellenberg. But he thought of those men, far away in England still — men he had not yet seen and perhaps never would, yet all the same, men like himself, outsiders, exiles in a foreign country, not belonging like he had never belonged — and suddenly he was shaking Schellenberg's soft hand and saying with more enthusiasm than he had ever expressed in his life before, '*Brigadeführer*, I'll do it!'

Schellenberg heaved a sigh of relief. 'I knew you would. I knew from the start,' he said with equal enthusiasm, and told himself that even in the fifth year of the war the average young German's foolish and fatal sense of romanticism had not yet been crushed. He had found another prime pigeon.

BOOK THREE: *PLAN OF ESCAPE — NUMBER THREE CAMP (APRIL 1944)*

'Sixty days to go'

CHAPTER 1

The little camouflaged Austin van stopped outside the high gate, made of barbed wire. 'Come on,' Jackson grunted and tugged at the handcuffs which bound them together. Awkwardly they clambered out of the van, while the driver lit a cigarette after the long journey from London, and Wolf caught his first glimpse of the 'Naughty Boys home' — Prisoner of War Camp Number Three. He knew from his briefing that before the war the grim looking, red-brick house had been a borstal. In 1939 it had been evacuated and remained empty until 1940 when the first German PoWs had started trickling in and it had been turned into a PoW camp. In 1943 its defences had been strengthened, its middle-aged guards replaced by A1 young men, and it had been turned into a top security camp.

Now the old house was enclosed by a double barbed-wire fence, three and a half metres high, guarded at intervals by stork-legged watchtowers in which Bren gunners were posted next to the searchlights. The twin fences were two metres apart, the space between filled with coiled barbed wire to a height of a metre and a half. Beyond lay the wooden barrack huts of the Italian PoWs, who provided the German camp with its services. Around it was another fence, but it was unguarded; for now the Italians were officially the Britishers' 'co-belligerents' and during daylight hours the Italians could come and go as they pleased, when they were off-duty.

As they crunched down the gravel towards the waiting sentry, Wolf told himself that beneath his feet there would probably be the seismographs, connected to the HQ building to the right of the camp, which would record any underground vibration caused by tunnelling. Camp Number Three, as he well knew from the briefing in Berlin, was very well guarded.

'Halt!' Jackson barked and jerked at his cuffs painfully. 'New boy,' he said to the sentry, a keen-eyed young soldier in khaki with the red flash of the Hampshire Regiment on his shoulder. 'Sign for his body, mate.'

The sentry duly signed. Jackson looked at the pale-faced officer whom he had so brutally beaten the night before. 'Ta ta, mate, see you after the war,' he said and smirked. Then he marched back to the van.

'Inside,' the sentry snapped, opening the gate.

'*Ich versteh' kein englisch*,' Wolf answered, appearing not to understand, knowing that his pretended lack of the language might serve him well in the future.

'Will you get in there, gildy!' the sentry jammed the brass butt of his rifle into Wolf's ribs.

Wolf staggered through the first gate and waited until the sentry had closed it behind them before passing on through the second one to the two men waiting for the new prisoner in the courtyard. One, Wolf could tell immediately, was a Jew. His swarthy face seemed totally foreign to the khaki battledress he wore so sloppily. The other, well over six foot, his eyes almost hidden by the stiff peaked cap of the guardsman, his square hard jaw a shining blue-black, was obviously a professional soldier.

'Stop there, you idle man!' he yelled, his words ending in a kind of scream. Even if he had not understood English, the long brass-bound stick which the man pointed at him conveyed the order with brutal clarity. Wolf stopped ten metres short of the strangely assorted pair.

The tall soldier, whose eyes still remained hidden beneath the peaked cap, raised his pacing stick. 'Tell 'im, Izzy,' he barked, as if he were addressing a parade fifty metres away and not one single shabby prisoner, 'tell 'im that, according to the Geneva Convention, I'm supposed to call him sir. But for me, he's nothing but Nazi scum. Put that in your funny lingo, Izzy.'

Corporal Bloom sighed and wished Sergeant-Major Hawkins would not call him 'Izzy'; it sounded so anti-Semitic, but he translated his words swiftly enough.

'Now all you lot in here,' the Sergeant-Major went on, 'are supposed to be a hard lot.' His dark face, which no amount of shaving and talcum powder could lighten and which had gained him the nickname of 'Black Jack' in the Grenadiers, contorted with scorn. 'But for me, yer a lot of softies.' With his good hand, he rapped the butt of the pace stick against his barrel chest. 'I'm hard — very hard, because I'm a bastard — a real bastard. In all yer life, you've never met a bastard like me. Tell 'im that, Izzy.'

Corporal Bloom told him.

Black Jack Hawkins pointed his big stick almost accusingly at Wolf. 'And I want yer to get this into yer square Hun head. Number Three Camp ain't one of yer Friday dinner fish and chip camps. Ner. It's bully beef and army biscuits here — every day of the week. Tell 'im Izzy.'

In spite of his words, which were almost comic, there was nothing comic about the soldier, Wolf could not help thinking. From those hidden eyes to the hand — it was missing three fingers — grasping the brutal stick, there was a latent, close-to-the-surface menace about the man. Wolf decided that he would be a bad man to cross.

'Now, one last thing,' the man was bawling at the top of his voice. 'I'd like to invite you to have a crack at escaping. My lads'd love it.' He pointed his stick at the nearest tower and involuntarily Wolf's gaze followed. 'In every one of 'em there's a first-class shot, with an itchy trigger finger, just dying to put a bullet in some heathen Hun.' He grinned evilly, but whether there was any answering light in those hidden eyes Wolf could not see. 'But mind yer, not quick. Something slow — a bullet in the guts or in the goolies. Something that would make yer suffer a lot. My lads'd like it a great deal. All right, Izzy, tell 'im that. Then get him over to Records; the MI Room for his check; then you can let him loose in the cage like the nasty Hun animal he is.'

And with that Warrant Officer Second Class 'Black Jack' Hawkins, veteran of Dunkirk, Greece, Crete and North Africa, where a German grenade had put an end to his fighting career and relegated him to the camps, marched away swinging his pace stick vigorously, shoulders rigid, as if he were still back at the Depot. Wolf had not yet seen those hidden eyes.

'*Heil Hitler!*'

'*Heil Hitler!*'

Wolf stood rigidly to attention in the door of the room, facing the *Ältestenrat* seated at the blanket-covered trestle table. From a room nearby came the sound of a reedy, scratched gramophone, playing an old pre-war favourite. There were three of them. The one with his right arm missing and dressed in a faded *Luftwaffe* uniform would be Ledig. Wolf knew from the Berlin briefing that Ledig was a personal friend of Göring's, shot down over the Channel in 1940. Göring had tried to get him exchanged via Sweden, but the English preferred to keep him as a kind of hostage. To his right, the tough-looking burly officer in naval uniform would be Commander Lott, a submariner, accused by the British of a war crime — his crew had allegedly machine gunned the survivors of a merchant ship they had torpedoed in the Indian Ocean. A very likely possibility for the plan, they had told him in Berlin. The third man, blond, young and bold-looking, wearing the ribbon of the Totenkopf, was an SS officer. He would be Berger, accused of helping to shoot one hundred British prisoners of the Norfolk Regiment in France in 1940. Another potential candidate, Wolf thought.

The three officers introduced themselves and then Lott began the cross-examination, without offering him a seat.

'*Oberleutnant* Wolf, it is our duty to ask you some questions. It is a matter of internal security. The Tommies are continually attempting to plant informers on us. You understand?'

'I understand.'

Lott turned to Ledig. 'Would you begin, Gert?'

'What was your squadron?' Ledig asked in the manner of a man who was used to giving orders and having them obeyed quickly. Wolf told him.

'You understand that, in due course, we can find out about you from comrades of the Hermann Göring who are in the Tommies' hands in other camps? We have a system.'

'*Jawohl, Herr Major.*' Swiftly, Wolf rattled off the names of ten pilots of the Hermann Göring who had been shot down the previous month.

Ledig was not impressed, Wolf could see in his small, suspicious eyes. 'That signifies little,' he said. 'Tell me who are the *Reichsheini*, Fat Hermann, Archer?'

Wolf told them, but they did not grin. Their faces remained hard and determined.

'Now you say you were a navigator?'

'Yes.'

'All right, how would you find north, if your instruments had been shot away, eh?'

'Would I have my wristwatch, sir?'

'You would.'

'Then I would point the hour hand in the direction of the sun and bisect the angle between it and twelve. That would give me the approximate south. Then —' Wolf rattled on, thanking God for the thorough training they had given SS cadets at Bad Toelz before the war.

Ledig grunted when he was finished and nodded to the other two. For ten full minutes they questioned him rapidly, snapping them out so quickly that Wolf realized this cross-examination had been well-prepared.

Suddenly Ledig broke in: 'Who is the Chinese?' he demanded.

'A fellow I met in my cell at Trent Park. He was washing socks…'

'Yes, he always is,'. Ledig interrupted him and now his voice seemed warmer. 'All right, why are you here?'

'Because I hit a British officer, one of the two who interrogated me at Trent Park.'

'What did you say?' the three of them exclaimed in unison.

'I hit a Tommy.'

'And what happened then?' Berger asked.

'They assigned me here and, on the night before I left, three of them came into my cell and did this.' Slowly and deliberately, knowing as he did so that, unwillingly, the Tommies had given him an ace, he took off his jacket and then his shirt. He raised his arms high so that they could see the green and blue bruise that stretched across his ribs and ugly red marks across his stomach. 'Beat me up.'

Ledig's eyes caught a glimpse of the little blue letter tattooed on the white untanned inner arm and knew instinctively that something was wrong. Then he, too, was around the table with the rest, shaking the new prisoner's hand heartily and slapping him on the shoulder, as if he were a long-lost brother.

'Well then, Wolf,' he asked, 'what can we do for you before we allot you to a room?'

'Yes, there's heaps of stuff here,' Berger said eagerly. 'Food, drink — we've got beer and homemade potato schnapps.'

Wolf grinned and shook his head firmly. 'No thank you all the same. I'm interested in other things than food and drink.'

'What, for instance?' Ledig asked, using the familiar 'thou'.

'Escape.' Wolf's voice was suddenly very determined. 'I want to escape from here at the first possible opportunity.'

CHAPTER 2

It was the evening of his second day in Number Three Camp. Wolf sat on the hard chair in the big low room to which he had been assigned by Ledig. On both sides of him towered the two-tiered wooden bunks with their straw mattresses. Above his head hung lines of washing which dripped constantly on to the bare concrete floor, the drops occasionally falling into the flickering, home-made lamp, making it splutter. But Wolf heard neither the light's noise nor the soft sounds of the others shuffling around outside. His attention was concentrated solely on Captain von Horn of the *Luftwaffe*, a tall, greying officer who had been captured in 1942 and would be accused of helping to plan the Coventry Raid if the British won the war. Von Horn was the last of the eight men he had picked in the forty-eight hours which had passed since he had arrived. But, as yet, neither they nor Captain von Horn knew that.

'You can go through the wire in many different ways,' von Horn was saying. 'In my time in the camps, I've seen men cut through, pushing a little sort of snow-plough in front of them to protect themselves from the coiled barbed wire. Others have tried to go over it — by pole, balloon, even a glider. A few have tried tricks. The chap from the *Kriegsmarine*, for example, who went out in the "night cart", up to his neck in sewage. Nobody could stand being close to him for a week after they recaptured him. But in the final analysis, where is your escapee going to escape to?' He looked pointedly at Wolf. 'England, after all, is an island, and no one — I repeat — *no one* German has succeeded in overcoming that particular problem in five years of war.'

For the moment Wolf left the question unanswered. Instead, he posed a question of his own. 'You have been in the camps longer than any of them. You're an old hand at this business what do you think of anyone's chance of escaping from this one?'

'Escape from here?' von Horn said. 'At first sight, impossible. There is no chance at all through the wire. That sergeant-major keeps the sentries in the towers and on the ground on their toes. They're more scared of Hawkins, I think sometimes, than a whole regiment of SS.'

'Tunnelling?'

'Out. They've got the seismographs working all the time and at night, just to make sure, they let the dogs loose. Whether it is just another of the kind of wild rumours which circulate in the camps or not, I don't know, but they do say the dogs are trained to go for one's sexual organs. Not a very nice prospect for someone of your age.'

Wolf agreed.

'However,' he leaned forward conspiratorially and indicated that Wolf should do the same, 'there is a way,' he whispered with his mouth close to Wolf's right ear. 'Indeed this very week two of our comrades are going to try it.'

'What?'

'Yes, Evers and Jahn, both completely crazy of course, are going to have a crack at it.'

'How?'

'A tunnel from the latrine,' von Horn answered.

'But you said that that was impossible because of the seismographs,' Wolf objected.

'I know. But they're doing it with a difference. They're not going directly outside. They're making their way first into the Spaghettis' compound.'

'And then?'

'And then, they knock a couple of Italians over the head, pinch their uniforms and say a very impolite goodbye to Camp Number Three.' He smiled, but his smile vanished as quickly as it appeared. Just then the bugle sounded its nightly call and Black Jack Hawkins' tremendous voice started to cry, 'Get those blackouts up everywhere! Come on, you idle Huns. Get them up!'

Captain von Horn said despondently, 'But even if they do pull it off, where in the devils' name are they going to go?'

Wolf had picked eight potential candidates. Lott, the U-boat commander, and Berger, the SS officer, were obvious choices. Ledig he had dismissed because of his physical disability — he needed completely fit men. Then there were the 'twins', as they were called in the camp, two inseparable young Marine lieutenants, captured during the Dieppe Raid and accused by the French of shooting civilians during the Raid, who, in spite of their obvious 'inclination', were bold and tough. Schulze was his fifth candidate. He was a beetle-browed bomber pilot, who had been nearly lynched after being shot down over the East End by a crowd of enraged cockneys and who, since then, harboured an implacable hatred of the English.

'Little Ali' and the civilian Hoehne had been six and seven. Both had been captured in North Africa: Little Ali (who was of mixed German-Egyptian parentage) while attempting to blow up Montgomery's HQ — the British regarded him as a traitor and he faced a court-martial after the war; and Hoehne at the great surrender of the *Afrika Korps* in 1943. Hoehne purported to be a war correspondent, but everyone in the camp knew that he was in reality a Gestapo officer, attached to the *Afrika Korps*. Von Horn had been number eight.

Up to the time von Horn revealed to him that the two officers, Evers and Jahn, were about to escape, Wolf had intended to explain his real purpose in the camp to the eight potentials immediately he had picked them. Now he decided to wait and see the outcome of the escape attempt. The way they had planned it interested him greatly. If they could do it, why shouldn't he and the men he had picked pull it off too?

On the afternoon of his fourth day in the camp the 'latrine rumour' passed from mouth to mouth, 'They're going out tonight'. That night Wolf could not go to sleep for a long time. He lay on his bunk, hands beneath his head, listening to the snores all around him, wondering how the two men were getting on. Had they already cleared the tunnel? Perhaps they were already in the Italian camp, searching for the chocolate brown battledresses the Italians wore, or a couple of Italians to knock on the head? Maybe they were already on the outside.

At midnight, still unable to sleep, he got up. He needed a drink. Slipping into his socks, he went out to the washhouse lit by a single, fly-blown bulb. But it was already occupied. Ledig, the one-armed Stuka pilot, muffled in a coat and blanket sat there, hunched under the light, reading a book. It was the Bible. Surprised a little, Wolf backed out unheard. He always respected those, who like himself, were alone.

Half an hour later he was asleep, dreaming of Maggie's broad, homely face.

The body count the next morning in the courtyard was completed surprisingly swiftly. There was no attempt to take a rise out of the Tommies by shifting around and refusing to answer one's name. The reason why was obvious. Lt-Colonel Hesketh, the bespectacled Camp Commandant, was taking the morning parade himself and that meant something of importance. Most of the prisoners thought it would be to announce the escape of the two officers. Lott, next to Wolf, nudged him and said, 'I bet he's peeing himself. Thinking they're going to send him to the front for letting them get away.'

Oberst Deschner, the senior German officer, saluted Hesketh and stood the German parade at ease. Followed at the regulation six paces by Hawkins and the scruffy little Jewish interpreter Bloom, the Camp Commandant stepped closer and cleared his throat nervously, his face grave. Hesketh, a peacetime accountant, had joined the Territorials in 1930 because 'one makes such good contacts' and because he liked wearing a uniform and carrying a sword on Empire Sunday parades. But he had never dreamed that he would ever be involved in a war. Even the stamp of Hawkins' boots on his office floor made him jump. Now someone had got killed and he didn't like it.

'Gentlemen,' he said, his breath fogging a little on the cold morning air, 'I have a t … tragic piece of news to ann … nounce to you.'

'This is it,' Lott said as Bloom translated.

'Yesterday night t … two of your comrades were shot while t … trying to escape.'

There was an excited buzz of chatter.

'Your comrades, Lieutenants Evers and Jahn,' the Camp Commandant continued, 'stole t … two Italian uniforms. But w … were caught half a mile outside the camp on the r … road to Winchester. My men ordered them to h … halt. They refused and,' Hesketh shrugged a little helplessly, 'they had to f … fire. They were killed outright. Please tell them that, Corporal Bloom.'

Wolf glanced at Hawkins, while Bloom translated. The Sergeant-Major's eyes were hooded, as ever, but there was no mistaking the look of triumph on his black face. He knew more about the killings than he had told his poor, helpless, ineffectual fool of a CO.

'Well?' Lott said, as they tramped away with the rest of the suddenly subdued prisoners, 'what do you think?'

Wolf considered his words very carefully before he spoke, watching a young PoW kicking a can aimlessly in front of him as he walked. 'They were shot half a mile from camp, that fool said, didn't he?'

Lott nodded his agreement.

'By guards from this camp?'

'Yes.'

'Well, what would our guards be doing so far away from the camp?'

'What do you mean?'

'I mean this.' Wolf lowered his voice. 'Those guards didn't just happen to be there; they were planted there and were waiting specifically for Evers and Jahn.'

Lott looked at him in alarm. 'You don't mean that...'

'I do. Someone betrayed them to the Tommies. Someone within our own ranks.'

CHAPTER 3

It had stopped drizzling. Now they exercised in the courtyard, with the grey rain-mist encircling their feet, as if they were walking through cottonwool. Round and round they trudged, just inside the wire, followed by the suspicious eyes of the lookouts. Some walked in groups — fours and fives — chatting about the latest war news. Others walked in twos, heads bent in deep conversation. A few walked alone, hands deep in pockets, heads sunk on their chests, swallowed by despair.

Wolf walked with his 'candidates', as he was now calling them to himself, completing circuit after circuit, chatting idly of unimportant things, while he wondered when exactly he should spring it on them. Finally he made his decision and, gathering the 'candidates' round him, he announced with surprising formality, 'Gentlemen, I am not what I seem. I have a confession to make.' He then rolled up his sleeve and raised his arm so that they could see the blue tattoo.

'You're SS!' Berger said in surprise. 'That's the blood-group mark. We all have it in the Armed SS. But in the devil's name, why are you wearing *Luftwaffe* uniform?'

Wolf rolled down his sleeve and lowered his voice slightly. 'Because I am an SS officer belonging to the Hunting Commando on a special assignment to this camp.'

'The Hunting Commando?'

'The Hunting Commando is a secret unit of the *Ausland-SD*, which carries out covert operations against the enemy. Sabotage, terrorism, assassination, kidnapping. The rescue of

Mussolini last year from his captors was one of our operations.'

Lott whistled through his teeth. 'But you don't mean you got in here *deliberately*, do you?'

'I do.'

The rest of them stared at him. 'But why?' von Horn asked.

For one moment Wolf hesitated. If any one of the eight 'candidates' were the traitor, he knew that if he answered that particular question he would be arrested — or possibly worse — within the hour. He took the plunge. 'Why? I shall tell you why, gentlemen. I have been sent here to encourage the boldest among the inmates to escape — and you are the boldest.'

'Good,' Berger cried enthusiastically. 'I'm all for that. But why send an agent to encourage us to do so? We all want to get out. But we can't get off the island, can we?'

'No, we can't,' Wolf agreed. 'But,' he hesitated and licked his lips. He hated to lie to these men, but he must, if he were to succeed in his own mission. 'It is not a question of escaping. It is a question of sacrifice — for Folk, Fatherland and Führer.'

'Sacrifice!' Schulze said angrily. 'What sacrifice can we make for the Führer in this stinking hole?'

Wolf stepped off the concrete onto what once had been an ornamental garden. With his right boot, he traced a line in the damp earth. 'The main road to Portsmouth on the English coast,' he said. He etched a thinner line to the right of it. 'The approximate position of Southwick House.'

'So?'

'So, this spring Southwick House is the most important building in the whole of England and it is only thirty kilometres from here.'

'And what makes this Southwick House so important?'

'It is the Headquarters of the Allied Invasion Forces,' Wolf said, lying easily now, 'and it is my mission to destroy it — with or without your assistance.'

'You see,' Wolf explained three hours later, while they crouched around him in the washroom, 'at the Hunting Commando we have decided that we can do nothing with the meagre resources available to us to stop the Invasion by ordinary methods. We decided, therefore, if we cannot strike at the legs or the guts, we must strike at the brain — and the brain is Southwick House. Already it is fully occupied by the enemy invasion staff. Montgomery is in residence, and with a bit of luck, we might have Eisenhower himself there when we attack. Imagine, therefore, what would happen if we destroyed the brains of the invasion in one stroke? It would put off their cross-Channel attack by weeks. The good weather of the spring would be gone and by the time they were ready to attack again under new commanders, our revenge weapons would have started taking a terrible toll on their cities and armies?'

'My God,' Hoehne said, speaking for the first time and looking at Little Ali, whose teeth were chattering with the icy cold of the washhouse. 'Germany could win the war after all.'

'Certainly. It would change the whole course of the war.'

Lott looked at Wolf. 'I have two questions. One, how do you propose to get us out of here. Two, even if we managed it, what would we use in the way of weapons to deal with this Southwick House of yours?'

'Let me take the second point first,' Wolf answered, lying easily now. 'One of our agents has already planted the explosive we will need for the job — and personal weapons, machine pistols — within one kilometre of Southwick House. Once we are out, we'll have the requisite supplies all right.

There is no fear of that. The answer to your first question is not so easy,'

'As you said yourself, the Tommies have electric devices under the earth to register any movement — so the only direction one can safely tunnel in this place is into the Italians' compound. That unfortunate business with Evers and Jahn showed that it could be done, however tragic the outcome. Now the latrine is out. But there is one other building which is much closer to the Italian compound and which is deserted from — say — six in the evening till five in the morning.'

'The Italian cookhouse?' Hoehne prompted.

'Right. Only fifty metres from their compound and used by them to prepare our meals, but only during the daytime. A matter of a week's tunnelling at the most.'

'But there's water seepage down there,' von Horn objected. 'We tried it out last year. You'd need plenty of wood to hold up a tunnel there.'

'What better place to find wood than a cookhouse,' Wolf answered. 'There's plenty of it lying around for the taking.'

'All right,' Lott said. 'But how are we going to hide the earth we take out? We can't rely on the Italians to help us. Those sparrow-eaters would betray their own mother to the Tommies for a bit of extra food, and we can't be running back and forth at night dumping earth. Not with those damn dogs out there. I certainly don't intend to end up singing treble.'

Wolf grinned. 'No, I can't let you risk that terrible fate, Lott. But I've thought of that one too.'

'How?'

'Every morning, each room sends an officer over to collect that brown hot water which the Tommies call coffee. Now if each room's officer took two jugs — we'll work out a reason why later — he could bring out one jug of coffee and one jug of clay, which the diggers of that night had ready for him.'

'Excellent,' Hoehne said. 'But doesn't that mean we run the risk of having our tunnel revealed to the Tommies?'

Wolf frowned. 'It is a risk we must take. I suggest the following: each one of you selects a comrade from each room, whom you can trust implicitly, to fetch the coffee each morning. Naturally the eight men selected will have to know there is a tunnel, but you will promise them that if they give us their help, they will be allowed to follow us once we are through.'.

'What about this as a suggestion?' Lott said thoughtfully. 'We pick only naval officers as the coffee-bearers and tell them that it is our intention to seize a fast motor-torpedo boat in Portsmouth harbour and try to get to France. We, the first party, will do the seizing, they will follow up — at a decent interval — to form the crew.'

'*Ausgezeichnet!*' Wolf said eagerly, realizing that he was not the only liar among them, 'and if they do get out and start flapping around, it can only do good. It will add to the confusion and cover our own purpose if they are caught and interrogated.'

'All right, one nasty question?' Schulze snapped, his face as angry as ever. 'How do we get in and out of the cookhouse at night with those damned hounds prowling around out there?'

'We don't,' Wolf answered.

'What the devil do you mean?'

'We smuggle ourselves in at supper and we leave with the coffee-fetchers in the morning.' He looked at the Twins. 'You two will ensure every evening that the Italians are occupied with other things than us.'

'Oh, my dear,' the blond twin sighed and fussed daintily with his hair. 'Not that. You don't know how hot-blooded those Spaghettis are!'

Wolf grinned.

'One last question,' Lott snapped. 'When do we begin?'

'Before I answer that,' Wolf said. 'Let me ask you one. How am I to inform Germany that I am here in this camp? I have a feeling that the Swiss Red Cross postcard is going to take an age.'

'It will. Up to six months, if the Tommies feel so inclined. No, the quickest way is to let yourself be used for one of those propaganda broadcasts the BBC does for the Reich from PoWs. You know: I'm well. The British are not bad fellows after all. They are treating me well, and the rest of that shit. Now, my question. *When?*'

'Tomorrow night.'

CHAPTER 4

'All clear,' Wolf whispered. 'He's off!'

The sound of the last Italian cook, his blouse undoubtedly full of stolen German rations, singing the Italian version of *Lili Marlene*, died away outside.

Wolf dropped out of the loft into the central cookhouse. One by one the others followed him. Hoehne came last and even the middle-aged Gestapo man managed the exit a lot better than he had seven days before. But since then he had lost ten pounds in weight and had acquired muscles 'I didn't even know I had', as he had confessed at the end of one back-breaking shift.

Swiftly they went into action, each knowing by now what he was expected to do. Lott and Wolf, socks round their boots to deaden the noise on the concrete floor, hurried over to the middle boiler, in which the Italians had cooked their thin midday soup. They reached under, noting that its base was still warm, and with a grunt lifted up the trap, which was a concrete slab. They had levered it out the first night and set it in a wooden frame for easier handling in the future. The sour smell of clay hit their nostrils, but by now they were used to it.

Little Ali crawled past them and turned on the lights. He had proved a tremendous thief and a tremendous improviser. In the upper floor of the old house he had discovered an unused signal-bell apparatus, which he had promptly stolen. The wires were old and worn and each joint had had to be wrapped in sacking to prevent the workers receiving shocks, but it had functioned well enough with stolen bulbs (protected by shades made of empty jam tins), strung along the length of tunnel.

Now it was the workers' turn. Schulze and Berger were working this shift on the face, with the Twins behind them to clear away the earth, which Little Ali would reach up to Wolf and Lott who would hide it for the morning coffee fetchers. Hoehne and von Horn, the least fit of the would-be escapers, dropped now into the hole and, squatting on the mud floor directly below, began working the air-pump, a concertina-like device made from stolen British Army canvas kitbags.

Wolf took a quick look round. Everything was all right. He raised his thumb in the English gesture. Lott grinned and repeated the gesture. *Southwick House Tiefbau GmbH*, as they had named their operation, could begin operations once more.

In the last seven days they had dug — at a depth of four metres — some fifteen metres due south straight towards the Italian compound. At first it had been easy going. Directly underneath the cookhouse they found light earth, mingled with a little clay, and they had cut it away in huge chunks. Indeed the only danger was that the soil was too loose. Everywhere in the first section, their shoring, made of firewood stolen from the cookhouse and the occasional bed board from their own beds, bulged ominously, and on every first shift it took the faceworkers a moment or two to overcome the panicky knowledge that there were four metres of earth above them.

On their fourth day of work they had hit clay. Now the back-breaking slog really began. Lathered in sweat, half-choked in the foul air, working in the shadowy, flickering light cast by Little Ali's electrical system, they hacked desperately at the clay wall in front of them with their knives. There was no sound save the faint hiss of the pump and the harsh gasp of their own escaping breath every time they stuck the knife home and dug out a fragment of clay. It seemed to take an age to fill a tiny sledge full of the stuff which the men behind would push to the exit. After a two hour shift under such conditions, the face workers would have to be hauled out of the trap, the long woollen underpants — their only clothing — soaked with sweat, their eyes blind with exhaustion, to lie flat on their faces on the concrete, gasping like men just rescued from drowning.

Yet they were making progress. On the sixth day a thin twig cautiously forced to the surface — after an hour's hard work — had been spotted and destroyed the next morning, only ten metres from the unguarded wire which separated them from the Italian Compound.

Wolf hated yet loved the work. Every night he had to force himself to get down the hole and crawl to the face to carry out his two-hour spell. Yet in the morning when they released themselves from the loft and mingled with the early coffee collectors, he longed to be back underground away from the hopelessness, the trivialities and squalor of the daytime camp.

On the seventh night of the *Southwick House Tiefbau GmbH's* existence, they finally broke through the layer of clay. At one o'clock in the morning they struck earth again. The sledges, now being hauled to the exit by ropes made of string taken from the Swiss Red Cross parcels and plaited together, began to appear with increasing speed. At two o'clock the Twins, who were at the face, appeared, exhausted but grinning. They raised their thumbs in the Tommy gesture of triumph and collapsed on the concrete floor. Lott and Wolf made their way up the tunnel, squeezed by Berger and von Horn who were in charge of removing the earth, and started to dig.

An hour passed. Wolf was just congratulating himself that they must have cleared at least half a metre in the last sixty minutes, when there was a hollow, ominous boom. The lights went out and instinctively Wolf threw himself backwards in sudden panic. Blindly, in total darkness, he backed on his hands and knees.

Suddenly he caught himself. He stopped, as if he had run into a brick wall. He heard his own voice command, 'Get the lights on up there — quick! There's been a fall!'

Further down the tunnel, von Horn flashed on his precious torch. By its light, Wolf could see Lott's legs, beating up and down frantically, as he struggled vainly to free himself from the thick heap of soil which buried his upper body.

'Hold on, Lott!' Wolf cried. He crawled forward and carefully grabbed Lott's legs. He pulled. Nothing happened. He pulled harder. The drizzle of earth became a thick rain. But Wolf knew he could not waste any more time. Lott was choking under that load. With all his strength, he pulled and Lott was suddenly free, choking and gasping for air, crying, 'Get out … get out … the whole tunnel is going to fall in!'

But the expected fall did not take place. Instead Wolf could feel cold fresh air striking his face from the side. He turned to Lott, the whites of his eyeballs shining against his black, sweaty face. 'Can't you feel it — air is coming in from somewhere?'

Lott wiped the earth from his face and said shakily, 'The only thing I can think of at the moment is that I thought I was going to look at the potatoes from below.'

Wolf patted the submariner on the naked arm affectionately. He had come to like Lott a great deal in these last few days. 'Just you rest here. I'm going forward again to have a look-see.' He raised his voice. 'And hurry up with those damned lights, can't you?'

He crawled forward and with his knees apart, began shovelling the loose earth between them and to his rear like a child does with sand on the beach. Above him he could feel a thin trickle of earth descending on to his naked back. But he was no longer afraid. His sole concern was to discover where the cold air was coming from.

The lights went on five minutes later. Wolf hardly noticed. Normally at the rate he was working, his heart would have been pounding like a trip hammer gone crazy by now. But not in the fresh air. He felt as if he could work for hours under such conditions. Finally he had cleared enough of the fall to continue. 'Pass me your torch, von Horn,' he yelled.

The precious torch, its battery already beginning to fade, was handed along to him. He clutched it and edged his way forward carefully. A small chamber had been opened up beyond the fall — perhaps a couple of metres broad — before the earth began once again. Curiously he flashed his torch beam around it, looking for the source of the fresh air.

He wriggled forward and felt the breeze directly on his naked back. With difficulty he turned himself round and flashed the weak yellow beam upwards.

A narrow chimney opened above his head and it was from there that the air was coming. Wolf held up the torch as far as he could, turning his head slightly to one side so that he could follow the beam. Then he saw it — just vaguely, but definitely there — a narrow shaft of stone and broken brick, through which the air came from above as if through a filter.

'*Brick?*', a little voice inside his head queried. '*Why bricks?*' Then he had it. It was the base of one of the concrete posts which held up the wire!

'We're under the wire,' he yelled at the top of his voice. 'Did you hear? We're under the wire! We've done it!'

And from what seemed very, very far away, Lott's voice came back, as calm as ever now, in a perfect imitation of the upper class English officer's drawl, 'Jolly good show, Wolfi, jolly good show!' And then in down-to-earth Hamburg German. 'But must you make so much row, Wolf? Remember you're on the BBC tomorrow.'

CHAPTER 5

'Bubble.'

Squadron Leader Taylor looked up and frowned. It was raining again and the bottle of scotch he kept hidden in his desk would only suffice to give him two drinks to keep him going over a long, wet Wednesday afternoon. 'Yes, what is it, Squeak?'

'What do you make of this?' Squeak was in a good mood; there had been a fried egg for breakfast and a piece of beef for lunch.

'Make of what?'

'Our pal Wolf has just done a turn for the BBC's German service,' Squeak answered, tapping the list on the paper in front of him.

Taylor looked up sharply, the whisky situation forgotten. 'What did you say?'

Squeak looked at the paper. 'Well, you see, I like to keep up with the doings of our graduates in their country residences, checking whether they're being good boys or not, and the BBC's tame Jerries of the propaganda department regularly let me have a list of PoWs who do the propaganda bit to the Homeland. For me it's rather like reading the school mag to check what the other chaps have been up to since they left. Well, I was reading the latest and what do my greedy little eyes see but this? One Wolf, *Oberleutnant der deutschen Luftwaffe*, broadcast a short message to his people in the jolly old Heimat.' Taylor looked at him incredulously. 'You must be joking? That feller would never fall for that tired old propaganda dodge.'

'Well, he did.' Squeak tapped the paper. 'It says so here in black and white.'

Taylor did not hesitate. He picked up the 'phone. 'Get me Crossman — yes — Dick — at the BBC.'

Fifteen minutes later the two Intelligence officers were pouring over the text of the recorded message which the evening service of the BBC had broadcast to Germany the day before.

'My name is Wolf, Lieutenant in the German Luftwaffe ... I was shot down last month over Dover ... I am well and un-wounded, Uncle Otto ... in the camp to which they have taken me, I am treated well and there is plenty of good food. To everyone else who hears this message, I say, that the time has come to end this terrible war. Many of my comrades in the camp think the same.'

'I just bet they do, especially in the Naughty Boys' Home!' Taylor said scornfully, dropping the message on his desk.

'Just the usual propaganda stuff,' Squeak commented, 'with the sting in the tail. They make them pay for their supper, over there in the Jerry Department.'

Taylor stared at the message thoughtfully for a few moments, then he said, 'Don't you think it's strange?'

'Of course it is. Wolf's not the type at all. Definitely a class-A, bloody-minded Jerry for my money. Why should he let himself be talked into anything like that?'

'More. What do you think the reaction to his message will be at the Naughty Boys' Home?'

'Agreed. He won't be the first Jerry who's disappeared into the camp bogs.'

Taylor got up and walked over to his filing cabinet. He pulled out the Wolf File and scanned through it. There wasn't much in it — in retrospect Wolf had been a remarkably tough baby; they had got very little out of him. But one thing was sure. His next-of-kin was listed as Gräfin von und zu Brahmsee, Wiesbaden, Kaiser Wilhelm Ring. There was no mention of any 'Uncle Otto'.

Taylor sat down at his desk again and lit his old briar. After a few moments it began to bubble. Tomm knew it well; it meant the Chief was on to something.

'Well,' he said at last, 'what is it?'

'I think it's about time we had our man from the Naughty Boys' Home up here.'

Agent 'Flyboy' was unlike most of the agents that the Twenty Committee recruited for their double-cross game during World War Two. Most of the top-secret intelligence organization's recruits were German agents who had been offered the old and final alternative, 'Either you work for us, or one dawn soon, they will take you and string you up by your neck in some prison yard.' Flyboy had not come to them like that.

One morning in mid-1942 he had walked into the office of the Commandant of Grizedale Hall PoW camp and, without any preliminaries, asked the astonished Commandant if he could not work for the Allied cause in any capacity — save one. He would not take up a weapon against his fellow countrymen.

He had been passed on to Intelligence and, in the end, Masterman of the Twenty Committee had let Taylor have him because Flyboy was, after all, an Air Force Officer. Thus he had come into RAF Intelligence. Right at the outset, Taylor had told him that he would do his best to ensure an early release for him after the war, but that if he were up to any kind of nefarious game, it would be very much the worse for him.

Flyboy wanted no favours and no rewards. He had volunteered to 'betray' (and he had actually used that word) his fellow countrymen because during the months he had been at Grizedale Hall he had undergone a religious conversion; he had come to realize that he had served an unjust cause; that he, too, had committed a crime when he had dive-bombed the Polish villages in '39, the French refugee columns a year later, and, in 1941, the British coastal resorts. He must now help — in the only way he could — to eradicate the 'cancer of National Socialism'. Back in 1918 when he had been imprisoned in Holzminden, Taylor had himself met one or two prisoners who, prior to their capture, had been bluff, ordinary, extrovert chaps, but who in the camp had withdrawn into themselves and had ended up by 'getting religion', as the phrase of the day had it. Thus he accepted Flyboy's reason for volunteering his services and his trust had been justified. The whole summer of 1943 Flyboy had worked at the Officers' Transit Camp No 13, between Alfreton and Ripley, where, in the guise of the Senior German Officer with a very sympathetic ear for the problems and uncertainties of newly captured officers, he had found out a great deal of information about the development of the Peenemunde Experimental Station and the new weapons being tested there.

That autumn Flyboy was transferred to the German Senior Officers' Camp at Enfield, suitably promoted to Colonel, where he found out a great deal about the *Wehrmacht's* planned assassination attempt against Hitler from the Camp's senior officer General Ritter von Thoma. Two months later, Flyboy, transferred now to Camp 7 on Lake Windermere, succeeded in finding out the details of a plot to organize all the prisoners throughout the United Kingdom so that when the Invasion started there would be a mass escape attempt to disrupt communications. The German officers concerned had been quietly moved to Canada. In order to maintain his cover

Flyboy had also been moved, transferred to the Naughty Boys' Home as 'a punishment', with orders from Taylor to discover what motivated the hard-core prisoners there in their resistance to the British authorities, when it was pretty clear that Germany had lost the war. Taylor needed the information for a project which was dear to his heart — the intended rehabilitation of key German PoWs to be released as soon as the war was over to help in the post-war democratization of their country.

Taylor knew that it had been a hard two years for Flyboy. Not only had he to face the prison atmosphere like the rest; he had also been confined in a prison within a prison — that of his loneliness and fear of discovery. Over the months Taylor had seen him transformed from a hefty man with dark hair to a skinny, greying creature, the left side of whose face twitched noticeably. But as Tomm ushered Flyboy in that morning, Taylor saw at once that he looked worse than ever. There were dark circles under his eyes and his face was a leaden-grey colour.

'My God, Ledig!' he exclaimed, 'what the devil have you been doing to yourself? You look awful!'

Ledig slumped down in the chair and said glumly, 'We have had a tragedy at the camp.'

'What tragedy?' Taylor asked.

'Last week two of the young hotheads escaped. I thought it my duty to report what they were attempting to do to the Camp Commandant — in the usual way.'

Taylor nodded. In order to protect Flyboy in case his life were threatened or if he had a really important message for RAF Intelligence, a yellow chalk mark on the inner gate indicated that there was a message hidden to the right of the left gatepost. Colonel Hesketh did not know from whom the messages came, but he did know that the messages were absolutely genuine and urgent; Taylor himself had briefed him on that.

'You see I wanted to have them stopped before they got out of the camp,' Ledig continued, his cheek trembling. 'With this Invasion build-up, and troops everywhere, especially the Americans, who seem to be very trigger-happy, I didn't want them shot bumping into some Army encampment.'

'But what happened?' Taylor coaxed him gently, realizing that he would have to sacrifice some of his precious whisky to calm the German down.

'They were shot, while attempting to escape,' Ledig said, and for a moment Taylor thought he was going to break down and cry. He reached under the desk and poured out a glass of neat whisky. As an after-thought he poured one for himself too. He pushed Ledig's glass across the desk and the German, snatching it eagerly in his left and only hand, downed it in one gulp

'An administrative mix-up, I expect, Ledig. These tragedies always happen in war?

'But they mustn't again! I do not do this work so that silly young men, not yet twenty-one, are to be killed in an ambush, Squadron Leader!'

'Of course you don't,' Taylor said soothingly and scribbled on the pad in front of him. 'I shall make a note of it. I shall see Hesketh about it personally.' He wouldn't, but he must appease Ledig; the man was very valuable to him. Besides he liked him. He decided then that if the pressure got too much, he would have him transferred again, perhaps to the London Cage. He would be useful there; Colonel Scotland would like him.

He poured Ledig another whisky and looked sadly at the empty bottle. 'Major Ledig,' he said carefully, knowing that one mustn't lead a witness, especially a friendly one, 'what do you make of *Oberleutnant* Wolf?'

'Who?' Ledig was still taken up by the death of the two young escapers.

'Wolf, a *Luftwaffe* navigator?'

'That one.' He looked sharply at Taylor. 'Why do you ask?'

Taylor told him and Ledig's frown deepened visibly. 'It is strange, as you say, especially to do a propaganda message in a camp like Number Three. Though, there has been no trouble about it — yet. And that again is strange. But I'll tell you something stranger, Squadron Leader.'

'Yes?' Taylor leaned forward.

'When your man Wolf took his shirt off on the day of his arrival in the camp, I could clearly see that he had the blood-group mark of the SS on his left upper arm. Now, what do you make of a *Luftwaffe* navigator who bears the mark of the Armed SS on his arm?'

'What indeed?' Taylor puffed hard at his pipe and it began to bubble steadily.

CHAPTER 6

The tunnel was nearly finished now. They planned to come out just beyond the first Italian barracks in order to have cover from the German camp. To make doubly sure, the ingenious Ali had discovered a way of short-circuiting the air-raid siren on the top of the old house. At the same time as they planned to break up to the surface, the simple time-device he had designed would activate the siren and all the lights would go out as they always did on the sounding of an alert.

While they had been digging, they had given much thought about the manner of their escape, once they were successfully through the wire. They had agreed almost immediately that they would not remain together for the first night, but would separate and meet again the following morning at a spot they had picked in a small wood off the Fareham-Portsmouth road, close to where Wolf had said the explosives were buried. The next day would be spent in a reconnaissance of Southwick House.

Each of the escapers had begun to prepare his own cover for the escape. They had decided they would not try to steal Italian clothing, as Evers and Jahn had; for as Schulze had said, 'Perhaps it was the Italians who betrayed them. Surely a German officer would not do such a dastardly thing?'

The Twins, who both came from the Frisian Islands and spoke a dialect that might pass as Dutch, had shortened their naval greatcoats, replaced the eagle on their caps with a fair imitation of a crown (made of silver paper obtained from the British cigarette packets the guards threw away) and hoped to pass as two Dutch petty-officers on their way back to

Portsmouth from leave in London. Little Ali, who spoke fluent English and was suitably dark, was a lascar seaman, returning to his ship, taking with him his 'mate' Hoehne, who had been struck dumb when their ship had been torpedoed in the Atlantic. Berger and Schulze were going to try their luck as Irish workmen, who were known to be employed in great numbers in England to make up for the men called into the Services. Their English was not too good, but they relied on the fact that the English themselves had difficulty in understanding the Southern Irish.

Von Horn caused somewhat of a sensation when he appeared in his disguise. With his skinny legs shaved and dyed with the tan that British women used to make up for lack of stockings in 1944, he was dressed in a short floral skirt (it had once been a curtain), tight, figure-hugging short jacket (made from a *Luftwaffe* tunic), his long hair combed down and peeping from beneath his bonnet (a dyed English stocking cap which the soldiers wore beneath their helmets) in a kind of Eton crop.

'Well,' von Horn said, 'the Tommies are less likely to stop a woman than a man.'

'Yes,' one of the Twins commented, 'especially if she looks like you!'

Commander Lott had given much thought to his costume. As he spoke fluent Russian, from his service on the Black Sea, he decided to go out as a Russian Liaison Officer attached to Southwick House Headquarters. His own blue uniform served as the base for his disguise as Captain Filov of the Red Fleet. The Russians wore the same ankle-length greatcoats and with the self-made red star on his cap and the pistol at his belt (the holster made of cardboard, burnished and blackened with shoe polish, the revolver laboriously carved out of wood and burnished and blackened in the same manner) Wolf had to admit he looked the part.

'You see,' Lott explained. 'It's the ideal way of getting into Southwick House. There are bound to be Russian observers there. The Ivans have their fingers in every pie. It should fool the average Tommy sentry at least.'

Wolf agreed.

'But what about you, Wolf?' Lott asked curiously. 'How are you going to doll yourself up?'

Wolf had been giving much thought to that problem himself. Once the escape became known, he knew the others didn't have a chance in hell of penetrating the coastal area — and as for finding the mythical store of buried explosives... Anyone wandering around the roads, speaking little English, as they mostly did, would be picked up at once. For him it was essential to get off the roads or to use normal transport, just as any ordinary Tommy would. But for that he needed the kind of cover which would take him automatically through every check — he needed a uniform.

But he didn't tell Lott that. Instead he said, 'Don't worry. I'll be well prepared on the day.'

The day was almost there and Wolf's cover lacked one thing only — an identity disc of the kind the British soldiers and non-commissioned officers wore on a piece of string around their neck. To obtain one he enlisted the aid of the Twins, who were completely incurious about anything and everything save their own bodies; they would not ask awkward questions.

The three of them wandered over to the cookhouse, to where the British corporal in charge of the Italian cooks was lounging outside in a vest, smoking a Woodbine.

'Hello, girls,' he said easily. 'Got yerself a new friend, eh?' He winked knowingly at the Twins.

The blond one flipped a wrist at him. 'Corporal Wright, how can you say such things about a German officer?'

'Give over,' the greasy-looking Corporal said good-humouredly. 'Everybody in the camp knows.'

The blond twin let him ramble on for a while, only half understanding the man's slang; then he posed his question. 'Corporal Wright, I know you English are prudes, but surely you don't go as far as putting your religion on your identity discs?' Wright looked at him, wondering if he was trying to get a rise out of him.

'What do you mean, Phyllis?'

'Well, my friend here says you do, and I've bet him ten cigarettes you don't.'

'He's wrong then,' the Corporal said, grinning. 'He's lost his ten fags because we do. Look.' He reached into his greasy vest and pulled out the two discs hanging on a piece of dirty string around his neck.

'Can we have a look, Corporal?'

'Sure,' Wright said and handed them to the blond Twin. He pointed a finger at the 'RC' stamped at the base of the discs and said in English. 'There you are. Wolf — RC; that means Roman Catholic.'

'That's right,' the Corporal agreed. 'Roman Candle — that's me religion — and right handy it is for getting off church parades in these parts, 'cos there ain't many Roman Candles around this part of the world.'

Wolf pretended not to be convinced and in German demanded to see the discs himself. His eyes took in the details — name, service number, religion. Then he clasped his hand over one of the discs very hard.

Seconds later, out of sight of the Corporal, he outlined the white impression the disc had made on the palm of his left hand swiftly with his pen.

It took him one whole morning to make a fake disc. He tried first with a piece of stolen linoleum. It had almost the same consistency as the real plastic disc. But it proved impossible to dye it the required red colour. Paper, even the thickest, turned out to be no good and in the end he compromised with cardboard. Admittedly it wasn't thick enough or stiff enough, but he slit the piece he had selected down the middle with a razor blade, inserted a flat piece of tin from a toothpaste tube and stuck the lot together with glue made from the sticky condensed milk the Swiss included in their Red Cross parcels. With the point of a sharpened nail file, he cut in the required details, before placing the discs on the cookhouse central heating to dry and harden. That morning when he came out of the tunnel to hide in the loft until the coffee-men came, he found the ink had dried perfectly. He had his two discs. Now he was almost ready to go.

It was Thursday. That morning while they waited in the loft, Wolf gave them the final briefing and they listened attentively, for now he had established his authority over them, although they were older than he and, in four cases, of senior rank. 'We shall set your timing-device, Ali, so that it goes off exactly at midnight on Saturday.'

'It will be done,' Ali said.

'That will mean we shall be leaving the tunnel at ten minutes after twelve. I'm hoping that it won't take us more than five minutes to cut the bottom strand of wire with the clippers.' He indicated the stolen garden clippers which they had spent hours sharpening on a stone for the specific purpose of cutting the wire. 'More we don't need to do — the way your figures have been reduced of late.'

They all laughed.

'Once outside,' he continued, 'we break up into our teams immediately. Each group or individual will stick to his allotted route — no deviation will be allowed unless it is a very serious emergency. Clear?'

'Clear.'

'Two hours after we have gone, the coffee-fetchers, who will remain concealed up here in the loft while we're down in the tunnel can make their break for it. It might even be wise to let them, in their turn, pick eight other trusted friends, who could attempt to get by the dogs and into the cookhouse before dawn and have a go themselves.' He hesitated for a moment. 'I know it's a terrible thing to do, but the more trouble the Tommies are faced with on Sunday morning, the better our chances are of getting away — and those eight officers and whoever else they find to follow them will be that trouble.'

The others nodded their agreement.

'Now, you all know what the Tommies are like? For them the war stops precisely at midday on Saturday and begins again on Monday morning at six — seven if they've got a hangover. So we can assume, gentlemen, that next Sunday the checks will be laxer than normal. All the same, each of you must be under cover in the wood near Portsmouth before — say — nine o'clock. By that time the Tommies will be starting to rouse themselves.'

He pulled a bottle of home-made potato schnapps out of his pocket and handed it to Lott, the senior officer present. 'There you are Commander, make the toast,' he said.

'Make the toast to what?'

'To the end of *Southwick House Tiefbau GmbH*. Tomorrow night it goes into liquidation.'

CHAPTER 7

But *Oberleutnant* Wolf was not destined to be present at the final liquidation of the *Southwick House Tiefbau GmbH* that Friday evening. Immediately after a rollcall, a camouflaged Humber staff car arrived at the Commandant's office to discharge Corporal Jackson.

Ten minutes later Black Jack Hawkins personally escorted Wolf out of the German compound, swinging his brass pace stick in his most majestic manner to hand him over to a grinning Jackson. Five minutes later, Wolf was in the car and on his way to Trent Park.

Taylor received him with Tomm and a pale-faced, bespectacled American who wore strange golden sphinx badges on his collar. He exchanged the usual pleasantries in that soft deceptive manner of his, before he said, quite badly, 'Wolf we are not satisfied with you.'

Wolf gave him a half-smile. 'I'm not particularly satisfied with you either, Squadron Leader.'

Taylor returned the smile and said, 'That is not exactly what I mean. We don't believe your story.'

Wolf's face showed no emotion, but inside his brain was racing. Had they discovered what his true mission in England was? And what had the *Ami* got to do with it?

'For that reason, we are going to give you a little test,' Taylor was saying gently. 'I know it is not quite legal under the terms of the Geneva Convention, but you can complain to the Red Cross representative the next time he comes to Number Three, which I believe will be some time in the summer of 1946.'

If there was supposed to be any humour in the statement, Wolf did not see it at that particular moment. His mind was too concerned with the test. Were they going to drug him after all? 'The test is quite harmless,' Taylor seemed to anticipate his unspoken question. 'And completely painless. The only pain involved would be if I had to request Flight Lieutenant Tomm here to make you agree.'

Squeak clenched his redoubtable fist and glared at the German in his most 'sour' manner, while the American, who seemed to understand German moved behind the two and revealed his apparatus. Wolf caught his sigh of relief just in time. It was a polygraph, a lie detector.

Calmly he let himself be connected to the machine, knowing exactly what to expect, confident that the secret training he had been given at the Hunting Commando would enable him to beat it. The lie detector, he knew, recorded the reaction of the brain, pulse and blood pressure to the questions posed by the expert. The first few questions would be unimportant, to establish on the graph what the suspect's reaction to them was — to discover a kind of norm; then would come the difficult ones, which should make the graph-line of a guilty person waver like that of a seismograph recording an earth tremor.

Wolf recalled Professor Dr Heinz's advice during the training sessions the Viennese psychologist had given them back at the *Jagdschloss*, the Hunting Commando's HQ. 'Every man has done something in the past of which he is ashamed, gentlemen. Some vile act such as rape, incest, sodomy, homosexuality, even *defilement of the Führer's holy name*! All of us fear that one day this terrible deed will come out into the open. Now this is what you must do if you are ever faced by the lie detector — you must immediately recall that terrible action in your past and imagine what would happen to you if it ever came out. Scare yourself completely with that overwhelming terrible possibility.' Thus they had been trained to imagine the possible outcome of their 'vile act' while the Professor had asked each in turn the innocuous questions which started off all polygraph interrogations, until in the end there had been no appreciable difference between their reaction to a question such as 'Germany might lose the war, don't you think?' and 'Confess you are an agent of the German Secret Service, yes?'

'Okay, I'm ready, if you're ready,' the American said. Taylor nodded, and the little man turned his attention to the wired-up PoW, crouching over his squared graph paper. 'I'm going to ask you some questions. I shall know immediately whether you are lying or not. So it is no use doing so.' The voice was authoritative and Viennese. Wolf smiled to himself and wondered for an instant if Professor Dr Heinz and the American might once have been colleagues; and then the questions started.

Wolf's mind raced to the defence. He had been seated next to the girl in the night train to Hamburg from Berlin in the winter of '42 — about seventeen, blonde, pink rosy cheeks, innocence itself in her neat BDM uniform. He had been in one of his black, 'lone wolf' moods. The Bodyguard had again suffered terrible casualties in the winter offensive and he had been given survivors' leave. But Berlin had proved a miserable disappointment. He knew no one there and no one wanted to know him, it appeared, and he hated to have to go to the whores on the *Kudamm*. Now he was on his way to Hamburg, wondering why he was going there, but knowing he must do something to get rid of that terrible black loneliness which swamped him.

He hated the girl right from the start because of her sweetness and the fact that she was going to Hamburg to meet her family, as she told him almost as soon as they got into conversation, babbling on about her mother and the children and all the rest of a world that was as alien to him as Mars. He was determined to seduce her.

Two hours later at Madgeburg, while the train stopped, all lights out because of an air raid on the city, he had taken her in the rocking, smelly lavatory. And afterwards she had cried helplessly because she was much younger than he had realised. He feared what the authorities would do to him, even though he was an SS officer, if they ever found out. Leaving the girl, still crying, he had jumped the train as soon as it slowed down to cross the bridge over the Elbe. He had drunk himself into insensibility for every night of his leave thereafter.

And now as the character of the questions changed, he thought of that terrible denouement in the swaying toilet, wallowing in the full horror of it, almost forgetting the questions themselves until he heard Taylor say, 'Doctor, ask him right out — what is his real purpose in this country?'

The expert posed the question and glanced immediately down at his graph paper, but what he saw there was evidently disappointing, for he frowned and looked pointedly at the two British officers.

Tomm said in English, 'What about the SS mark Flyboy spotted?'

'Shut up!' Taylor snapped. But Wolf had heard enough, for as he told himself on the journey back to the camp from London after the completion of the lie detector test, two things were now very clear. One, his time was running out; the Tommies were on to him. Two, there had only been one *Luftwaffe* officer — and surely 'Flyboy' must mean an Air Force officer? — in the little group who had interrogated him on his first day in the camp, one who, in addition, had been called to Trent Park like himself the previous week. And that officer was Major Ledig. Now he knew who the traitor was at the Naughty Boys' Home!

They murdered Major Ledig immediately after roll-call on Saturday morning. Wolf knew that he could not afford to take any chances at this late stage and told Lott.

Lott immediately convened a 'court' and had Ledig 'tried' in the big outside latrine.

At first, pale-faced and terrified, he pleaded his innocence. It was just a co-incidence that he had been taken to Trent Park before Wolf. But when Wolf told Hoehne, who was doing the cross-examining, to ask him who 'Flyboy' was, Ledig broke down completely. He babbled on about the past, how he was doing God's work and was trying to protect them from themselves, saving them for a better life after the war. In the end Lott ordered him to be gagged, while the court made its decision.

'Guilty or not?'

Every hand went up.

'The sentence?'

'Death!'

The long wooden seat of the 'forty-eighter' — the longest latrine, which could take forty-eight men in a line — was taken off. Lott looked down into that awful pit, which was drained by the Italians once every three months, and gagged audibly. 'All right,' he said, 'bring the traitor over!'

A dozen rough hands hauled Ledig, now bound and gagged, towards the open latrine.

'In with him!' Lott commanded.

The men lifted Ledig high above their heads, and dropped him into the liquid mess. Ledig went in with a great splash, his scream stifled by the gag. In a moment he had disappeared from sight.

Swiftly the men replaced the lid of the 'forty-eighter' and hurried out into the bright May sunshine, blinking a little in its sudden glare. Two hours later, they were sealed up in the loft, with the eight coffee-fetchers who were to follow them down the tunnel.

They were on their way.

CHAPTER 8

In the loft they were pulling on their striped camp pyjamas, watched by the other eight who would follow them through the tunnel. The pyjamas were to keep their disguises clean. Lott looked at Wolf, who was still dressed in his *Luftwaffe* uniform, though he now wore a pair of British Army ammunition boots. 'Are you going like that?' he whispered.

'Don't worry,' Wolf answered. 'I have my stuff waiting for me.'

Lott shrugged and continued struggling into the too tight pyjamas, while Wolf walked to the corner of the loft and, with his back turned to the others, unscrewed each of his five buttons in turn to reveal the money hidden there — four single English pound notes and one fiver. He smoothed them out, noting that the big white five-pound note already had a couple of signatures on its back, and put them carefully in his pocket, next to a safety razor and a sawed-in-half boot-brush — his 'escape gear'.

Then they were ready.

'*Hals und Beinbruch!*' the officers who were to remain called softly, as Wolf opened the trap. They returned the greeting and one by one dropped to the cookhouse floor.

All was still. The drunken carousing from the Sergeants' Mess had now died away and the only sound from outside was the steady pad-pad of the dogs in the compound and the sharp crunch of the sentries' boots on the gravel. Swiftly they crawled into the tunnel and took up their positions with Lott and Wolf in the lead. Ali remained behind at the lights, ready to douse them as soon as they could safely start working.

Nobody manned the pump this night; it was too strenuous and they would need all the energy they possessed before the night was out.

Half-an-hour passed. The tension was terrible. Wolf, lying on his stomach next to Lott, could hardly believe that in thirty more minutes they would be free. But the lack of air, without the pump, was getting serious. Wolf began to fight for breath and wondered how much longer he could stand the claustrophobic closeness of the tunnel.

Then it was midnight. If all was running smoothly, the siren would be now sounding up above, the lights on the wire would be flicking off and more sentries would be tumbling out of the guardhouse to their posts. 'Out lights!' Wolf commanded, 'Pass it back.'

'Out lights … out lights!' the command ran down the tunnel from mouth to mouth and suddenly they were in total darkness. Lott and Wolf seized their knives and began to hack at the remaining soil between them and the football pitch, the earth raining down on their heads, covered by old stockings. The first faint breaths of cold air began to filter down to them. Suddenly a big piece of earth came away and landed squarely on Lott's face. They were through!

Hurriedly they scraped away enough earth to allow a body through.

'You first, Wolf,' Lott whispered.

'All right!'

He put his hands on the edge of the hole and heaved himself up gently as far as his waist. Behind him, the Italian hut was silent, but to his right, perhaps twenty metres or so away, he could hear the steady tramp of a sentry. But he couldn't see him. The lights had gone out. Ali's device had worked perfectly. They would probably have half-an-hour or so before the Camp's Duty Officer discovered that there was no air-raid and the siren had gone off due to a 'short circuit', as he would probably phrase it in his report until morning roll-call showed him just how wrong he had been.

Wolf heaved again and pulled himself out of the hole altogether. From below there came the sound of falling earth. He flung himself on the ground, his heart beating furiously, head cocked to one side so that he could hear better. Surely the sentry must have heard the racket he had just made? But the steady crunch of heavy, hob-nailed boots on gravel continued undisturbed.

He waited no longer. Not running, but bent double and picking his way carefully across the pitch, making hardly any sound in his stocking covered boots, he headed for the wire. He flopped down near the post they had picked to assemble for the wire-cutting, just as the sentry came by and almost surprised him. He hugged the ground, face close to the earth so that no trace of white might betray him. Surely the man could not help but see him? But the sentry passed within three metres, whistling softly as he stamped by, and disappeared into the darkness.

Five minutes later, Lott was at his side, helping to cut through the wire with the improvised wire-cutter. Ten minutes later, they were all through and hidden in a little group of trees, some fifty or sixty metres away from the camp. Wolf, listening to them whispering to each other in the midst of an enemy country, with every man's hand against them, felt for them. They had been good comrades, but he would never see them again; for he knew what his fate would be once they found out about Ledig. The Tommies would attribute the murder to him and that would be that. They, for their part, would be recaptured and perhaps survive the war to tell their children one day about this strange lunatic adventure in wartime England — and the kids would probably laugh at them for being such fools. He said in a low voice, 'If you lot don't want to be back in there soon, you'd better get moving — *now!*'

'Of course,' Lott said and, with surprising formality, shook his hand. 'See you tonight, *Hals und Beinbruch!*'

'Same to you.'

And then they were gone.

Wolf had been watching Sergeant-Major Hawkins for days now. He knew his gait; he knew the way he never looked down, as if nothing would ever deign to bar his majestic progress; he knew the manner in which he turned his head when he suspected somebody or something was wrong, slowly and menacingly, as if his neck was worked by a series of rachets. He had studied his habits too — the way he came out of the Sergeants' Mess after lunch; from the roof of the old house he had been able to observe it clearly — wiping the back of his hand across his mouth, as if his dinner had been more liquid than solid; the regularity with which he went to the Mess each evening; and the fact that he never appeared at the Sunday morning roll-call, leaving that to Corporal Bloom. From which Wolf concluded that Hawkins allowed himself a 'real piss-up' on Saturday night and slept in late the following morning.

At that particular moment Wolf hoped he was right, for just then he was softly opening the door of the hut in which Sergeant-Major Hawkins lived in solitary splendour. The heavy, open-mouthed snoring coming from the bunk in the corner and the way the left arm hung over the side of the bed indicated that Hawkins was well and truly 'three sheets in the wind'. He would present no problems.

Ten minutes later, dressed in Sergeant-Major Hawkin's second-best battledress, Wolf strode down the blacked-out road towards the station. He was whistling.

BOOK THREE: *THE ESCAPE —*
SOUTHERN ENGLAND
(MAY, 1944)

'Thirty-six days to go'

CHAPTER 1

'Bubble!'

Taylor felt a hand shake his shoulder and groaned.

'Bubble — for Chrissake, wake up!' Squeak's voice was insistent.

'Go away,' he said, still keeping his eyes firmly closed. 'It's Sunday, damn you!'

'Bubble, will you damn well wake up, or do I have to pour the piss-pot over your drunken head?'

Weakly Taylor opened his eyes. Squeak, dressed in his best uniform, pistol at his waist, and with the armband of the duty officer round his right arm, wavered before his eyes.

'What's up?' he croaked.

'Everything,' Squeak snapped.

'Oh, well, that's all right.' He closed his eyes and muttered, 'I've decided not to go to church parade this morning. I've just become a Buddhist.'

'For crying out loud, man. The sodding balloon's gone up. they've escaped.'

'Eh? Who's escaped?'

'There's been a mass break-out from Number Three.'

Taylor sat up abruptly and wished next moment he hadn't: two red-hot steel prongs were being driven into his eyes. He groaned and held his head. 'What did you say?'

'There's eighteen to twenty PoWs missing from Number Three.'

'Oh balls. Squeak, I've got to have a drink. I can't function without one. Do you…'

'Yes, of course. But you know it's only ten thirty and I've only got gin and nothing to mix…'

'As long as its seventy percent proof, Squeak, I don't care if you mix it with gnat's piss.'

A few minutes later Squeak returned with his tea-mug, filled with gin and water, and watched anxiously as Bubble drank it, using both hands, which trembled like leaves.

'Now then, tell me that again — slowly,' Bubble said, his voice under control and the shakes gone.

'At roll-call this morning, they discovered that nearly twenty prisoners were missing from Number Three, including our friend Wolf.'

'And Ledig? What did he have to report?'

'Nothing.'

'What do you mean — nothing?'

'He went with them.'

Taylor looked at him aghast. 'Ledig wouldn't have gone with them unless they forced him,' he rapped, his mind functioning now. 'Or perhaps he didn't. Listen Squeak, I know in my bones that that feller Wolf is behind it all. I can't explain it rationally, but he is.'

'What do you mean?'

'I don't know exactly. But he's a plant. He isn't what he purported to be when we interrogated him. Where are those Germans going to? *Nowhere*! But for some reason Wolf could convince them that they should escape, although they knew as well as he did that they didn't have a hope in hell. But Ledig…' He bit his lip and drank the last of the gin and water. 'Squeak, get me a staff car and a duty permit.'

'But you're not on duty!'

Hurriedly Bubble got up from his rumpled bed.

'I am now,' he said firmly, opening the drawer of his bedside table and taking out his false teeth. 'After all, Ledig is our man.' '*Was*' would be better, the little voice at the back of his brain said, but he ignored it.

'Where are you going?'

'To Number Three, that's where.'

Colonel Hesketh was very upset. He had not been so upset since 1935 when his daughter Laura had confessed she was three months' pregnant by a dance-band saxophonist.

'M ... My God, Squadron Leader,' he protested to Taylor, who was dressed in his best uniform, with a .38 stuck in the holster at his belt, 'I've always t ... taken the most stringent security precautions, haven't I, Sar'nt-Major?'

'Sir!' Hawkins barked, enjoying the little prick's misery.

Taylor ignored Hesketh's protests. 'You say you had no signal from Flyboy?' Even now he was careful not to betray Ledig's identity. One never knew.

'No, I checked personally two hours ago, just to make sure. There was no chalk mark.'

Taylor nodded. 'Could I see the one you've got. We might get a lead out of him?'

Hesketh looked at Hawkins.

'Sir!' he bellowed at the top of his voice and marched out.

The young German, a ludicrously dyed civilian cap on his blond curls and a dirty raincoat covering his pilot's uniform, came hobbling in, disdaining the guard's aid, his face pale with pain.

Taylor nodded to Hawkins, who shoved a chair at the escaper; he had twisted his ankle a mile out of the camp and had been captured almost immediately after the alarm had been raised. 'All right,' Taylor said at once. 'You're in serious trouble, young man, and you know it. So I'm not taking any rubbish from you. I want the truth and I want it fast.'

Taylor had an instinctive feeling that something terrible had happened to Ledig and that the young man had been involved in it. The threat worked. The German grew even paler. Taylor grabbed the boy by his lapels. 'Now look, I want to know this. Where are they going?'

The boy hesitated. Taylor increased the pressure and glared at him.

'Portsmouth.'

'Where?'

The boy repeated the name.

'Why?'

'The others said that they were going to grab a ship there and try to escape to France. There were several sailors among them.'

Taylor laughed in his face. 'You must be mad! How the devil did you expect to escape from one of the most closely guarded harbours in the United Kingdom and get through the Channel?'

He stopped. There was no use going on at the boy; he was confused enough as it was. He swung round on Hesketh. 'Get on the blower, Colonel. Contact the head of the search group. They're heading for Portsmouth.'

In spite of the fact that he was senior to Taylor in rank, Hesketh obeyed at once. But before he picked up the 'phone, it rang.

Hesketh sprang to attention at the 'phone, as if the King himself had just entered the room. 'Yes sir,' he barked.

Taylor looked at him.

Again Hesketh said, 'Yes sir, of course sir. I'll send a truck and some of my people at once, sir. Thank you, sir. Yes sir!' Then he hung up.

'Who was that, Colonel?' Taylor asked. 'Not God by any chance?'

'It was General Belchem, reporting that they had rounded up a large group of escapers at the HQ just outside Portsmouth.'

'And pray who is General Belchem?' Taylor asked in his most arrogant tone.

Hesketh's stutter came back with a vengeance. 'He's C … Chief of Administration to G … General M … Montgomery.'

Taylor's mouth dropped open and behind him Black Jack Hawkins said, 'Oh, my red and rosy arsehole — *Monty*!'

CHAPTER 2

'So I thought this is really rather strange,' the General said, swinging his golf club back and forth easily. 'What are these chaps doing skulking around in the shrubbery? What?'

Taylor standing rigidly to attention in front of the General, who wore a black Tank Corps beret, a scruffy khaki pullover without any badges of rank, grey corduroy civilian trousers and — quite incongruously — golf shoes, gulped and said stupidly: 'Yes sir!'

The General swung his mashie niblick once more. 'I mean, one can't have chaps like that, putting one off one's stroke, can one?'

'No sir!'

Montgomery, the Commander of the Invasion Land Forces, beamed at him, as if he were used to dealing with idiots and could tolerate them on Sunday mornings at least, when he had been to divine service and could relax over a little putting. 'So I walked over and said to them, "Now then, what are you chaps in those rather funny clothes doing in my back-garden, eh?" And by Jove, with that, the whole bunch of them start to come out of the shrubs with their hands up — like Tripoli all over again, what?'

'Yessir!'

'One of them is dressed up like a woman, but he's got no knickers on,' he laughed, 'or so my young chaps tell me. I'd really rather not look.' He laughed and pointed his golf club at the bedraggled von Horn in his dangling, wet, torn skirt, sitting miserably in the middle of the rest of the prisoners, guarded by Montgomery's 'young men'.

'Yessir!'

'Well, I'll be off now,' Montgomery said. 'See your chaps don't let them run away again, won't you? Can't have a lot of Huns cluttering up my HQ, can we now? Must have a really tidy show all the time, what?'

'Yes sir!' Taylor snapped, still standing rigidly to attention.

'And by the way, Squadron Leader, we mustn't drink when we're on duty, must we?' He gave Taylor a flash of his cold-blue eyes and then he was gone, swinging his club as he went, the whole incident wiped from his mind for good.

Taylor breathed out hard and relaxed for a moment. That 'we mustn't drink' business was in the best traditions of Trent Park — a real old sting in the tail. Then he brought his mind back to the matter in hand.

'Hawkins!'

'Sir!' Hawkins' voice was not quite its usual self; there was a note of awe in it, as he watched the scruffy little General disappear over the nearest rise.

'Get all of them over into the truck except...' Taylor's eyes lighted on the one who wore the uniform of what seemed to be the Red Navy, complete with dirk, obviously made out of wood, 'that big sailor chap there. I want him.'

'Sir.'

Taylor let them get on with it and walked over to the thin Captain, wearing the dark-brown beret of the 11th Hussars, who was commanding the mixed party of British and American officers, guarding the PoWs.

'Do you think you could do two things for me Captain?'

'Certainly.' The officer lowered his revolver, as the bedraggled escapers began to file towards the truck.

'Could I have the use of a room to interrogate that one.' He indicated Lott. 'It's very important. And then a telephone?'

The young Hussar officer said, 'You'll have to come over to the house. The General would have a fit if I let you use his caravans.' He indicated the three caravans fifty feet aways. 'They're holy, you know.'

He smiled and Taylor smiled back. He recognized the caravans too, from the newsreels of the desert fighting. Together they walked to the big house, with Lott limping in front of them, looking completely absurd now in his disguise. Taylor felt some sympathy for him. Years ago he must have looked the same to the fat Dutch border-policeman in what he had fondly imagined was a German working man's dress.

Although it was Sunday and the General himself had taken the afternoon off, the place was a hive of activity. Staff officers, with red tabs on their collars', clerks, hands full of documents, dispatch riders in ankle-length raincoats and crash helmets under their arms were coming and going all the time. 'Operation Fortitude, you know,' the officer said. 'Excellent idea, but it causes us a devil of a lot of extra work.'

Taylor nodded. He knew about the great deception, by which all the signals from, Montgomery's HQ were transmitted by landline to Kent and sent from there so that the Germans believed his invasion force would set out from there, heading obviously for the *Pas de Calais*.

'So I imagine,' he agreed, as the other man opened the door of a small, empty room and said, 'Use this. I'll stand guard outside. Though,' he looked at Lott, 'I don't think the Boche is going to do much running away again at this particular moment, do you?'

'No, I don't.'

'Shout out when you want to use the 'phone. You'll have to use the outside civvie line.'

'Thank you. I will.'

Taylor glanced round the room and then motioned Lott to a chair in the corner, while he dragged up another chair to face him. It wasn't the best way to conduct an interrogation — one should always establish one's superiority right from the start — but it was all he had. He asked the man's name and then, as an afterthought, gave him a cigarette. He didn't look a bad type, but was obviously beat by the failure of his escape attempt.

'Now Herr Lott, who put you up to this ridiculous venture?'

Lott hesitated only a moment. After the first shock of discovering there was no hidden explosive and that Wolf was not going to turn up, he knew that they had been tricked. For hours they had wandered round the Hampshire countryside wondering what they were going to do and in the end they had almost been glad when the little General had routed them out of the bushes. Of course, Wolf had tricked them.

'Wolf,' he answered wearily.

Taylor looked at him sharply. '*Oberleutnant* Wolf?'

'Yes.'

'And where is *Oberleutnant* Wolf now, Lott?'

Lott shrugged wearily. 'Don't ask me! I saw him last just after we got under the wire.'

'Where do you think he's gone?'

Again Lott shrugged. '*Weiss nicht.*'

Taylor tried a new tack. 'All right, what was the purpose of your escape? I mean, any fool would realize after five minutes' consideration that there is no way off this island. Not one German PoW has managed it in five years of war!'

'We knew that,' Lott agreed. 'Wolf made the point right from the start. But you see Wolf had a plan for us.' Slowly he explained their plan, ending miserably with the words, 'and we couldn't even find the right house. This isn't Southwick House, is it?'

'No, it isn't,' Taylor answered slowly, letting the information run through his brain. Wolf had been deliberately planted in the Naughty Boys' Home, that was for certain. Perhaps it explained the mystery of the pilot's suicide and it certainly did explain why Wolf had flung a punch at Squeak; he had to be sent to that camp! But why all the trouble and the planning in order to lead a crazy raid on Southwick House, when Wolf knew from the very start that there were no hidden explosives?

'Are you sure you don't know which way Wolf went?'

Lott shook his head. He was slowly shaking off his sense of failure and the despondency which went with it. Wolf had tricked them, but he must have tricked them to some purpose. Their mission had been to fool the Tommies, to blind them with sand, create havoc and confusion in Southern England — and he, stupid fool, had suggested that the coffee-fetchers should be used for that purpose, while Wolf carried out the *real* one. Somehow he must protect Wolf, whatever his mission might be. 'I've told you all I know,' he said stubbornly.

Taylor took a chance. 'And what about Ledig?' he asked softly, looking at the man from the side.

Lott blanched. 'What do you mean?'

'Major Ledig is not in the camp, nor is he with you or the other escapers. He can't have vanished into thin air — and I know from another of your comrades that he was not in the original escape plot.' Taylor did not know, but he lied expertly. 'Now,' he said severely, 'I'm prepared to forget about Ledig for the time being, if you are co-operative. Well?'

'What can I tell you? I've told you all I know.' Lott said miserably.

'Little things,' Taylor said. 'You say you last saw Wolf at the wire. All right, which way did he set off?'

Lott thought. 'He was behind me, but he didn't set off south like the rest of us, I'm sure of that. It all happened so quickly.' Lott's brow creased in mock concentration, knowing that every minute he held Taylor here might help Wolf, whereever he was. 'I had the impression ... that he was going back to the main camp.'

'Back?' Taylor exclaimed.

'Yes.'

'But why?'

'Am I Jesus?' Lott shrugged carelessly. 'Perhaps it was something to do with his escape costume. He was still in *Luftwaffe* uniform, whereas we had...'

'What did you say? He didn't have any disguise like you others?'

'No.'

'My God,' Taylor said in English and to no one in particular, 'What the hell is going on here?'

Squeak asked the same question when Taylor called him on the 'phone five minutes later. But by the time Taylor had collected his thoughts and could say, 'Something very devious, that's for sure. But let me put it to you as simply as I can. One — Wolf was deliberately planted on us, a cuckoo's egg, if you like. Two — the whole escape business was stage-managed to throw dust in our eyes, alarm the countryside while Wolf went off on his own. Three — we can safely assume that because the subterfuge was carried out within the prohibited coastal area that is where Wolf is now. Four...'

But Tomm beat him to it. 'Four, what nasty little game is he up to there?'

Taylor was about to confess that he didn't know, when it came to him. That long-forgotten episode in Goethe's *Campagne* suddenly flashed through his mind, when the *Meister*, viewing the Prussians and Austrians streaming back in disorder before the guns of the French revolutionary rabble at Valmy, realizes that the brief cannonade on that sodden French field would change the face of the world. It was such a moment for him, standing there in the telephone box outside Montgomery's HQ, with the despatch riders roaring by in a constant stream on their muddy Nortons.

'His game? I'll tell you, Squeak,' he said, sure that he now had the right answer to the Wolf mystery. Then he said, 'But that presupposes one thing.'

'What?'

'That he has some means of getting the information out of the country and we know that he had nothing on him of that kind. In addition, we know there is not a single German agent still operating in the South of England. Special Branch has nabbed them all; they've long gone for their last outing at Wandsworth. There has been no illegal radio traffic in this part of the world since the autumn of 1943. The only W/T traffic with the *Abwehr* and *Ausland-SD* since that time has been by courtesy of the Double Cross Boys.'

'You mean the Twenty Committee?' Taylor said a little gloomily, fearing that his theory might not be so watertight after all.

'Yes. And even that has been stopped since the first week of February — just in case. Masterman was concerned lest one of his boys might just do a triple switch and earn himself the Knight's Cross by passing on info about the Invasion.'

Suddenly Taylor had an idea. 'Listen Squeak, do me a favour. Get on to Masterman, or any one of the Double Cross chaps you can find on a Sunday afternoon, and ask if you could have the details of any of their boys operating, or shall we say who used to operate, in this part of the world.'

'But they wouldn't give me information like that. To a lowly Flight Lieutenant!'

'Then do your Wingco act!'

'Of course! "Hello, this is Wing Commander Taylor, commanding RAF Intelligence, Trent Park here."' Tomm's voice went down an octave and became as fruity and full of gin as the real Wingco's. '"Use the scrambler, I'd like to ask you for some information…" Okay, Bubble, Wingco it is!'

Squeak called back an hour later. Outside the General's 'eyes and ears', as the General called the young men of his personal staff, were assembling on the lawn to take tea with the Master. There were piles of what looked like potted meat sandwiches and some sort of buns with currants, and big urns of tea. Taylor licked his lips. He fancied a drink too, but not of tea. Then the 'phone rang and he forgot his thirst.

'Worked like a charm,' Squeak said triumphantly.

'And?'

'Not a sausage.'

'What do you mean?'

'Well, the Double Cross Boys have put all their double agents in the Cooler till after the Invasion. They're taking no chances. There is only one Twenty Committee chap left in the whole of Southern England and he got burnt in 1942.'

'Burnt?'

'Yes, the heavies of the *SD* tumbled to the fact he was working for the Double Cross Boys then and struck him off their list as a very naughty boy.'

'Hm.' Taylor pulled a face. 'And why did they leave the blown one in place?' he asked.

'Oh, because he's some sort of vicar or other, I gather,' Squeak answered. 'He has a parish to mind.'

Taylor sniffed. 'Balls!' he said.

CHAPTER 3

It had been easy. Wolf had caught the night train from London and taken a third-class ticket to Exeter. At Dorchester he had got out. The station sign had been missing since the German invasion scare of 1940, but a porter had called out the name of the station obligingly enough and he had got up from the toilet, the only place where he had been able to sit in the crowded overnight train, and got out. The old man at the barrier had not even noticed that his ticket had been stamped Exeter.

For a moment he stood in the yard behind the station wondering what to do next. The few civilians who had got off the train lined up obediently at the bus stops, while a bunch of American servicemen stormed the waiting trucks, already decorated with the white star of the Invasion forces. Dorchester was just on the edge of the fifteen-kilometre area and somehow he must get through whatever guards the Tommies might have south of the town.

Then he spotted what he sought. One American truck stood apart from the rest. And he soon saw the reason why. Its driver was black. Obviously the man had been sent to the station to pick up any of his compatriots who might have arrived on the train. There was strict segregation in the US Army. White American troops would not travel in the same truck as black ones.

Wolf made a decision. He strode imperiously across the station yard, pushing his way through the white Americans as if they did not even exist and rapped on the door of the truck.

'Hey, there, laddie,' he barked in a passable imitation of Hawkins, 'you going to the camp?'

The driver looked down at this apparition in British uniform. 'What you say, Captain suh?' he gulped.

'Asked if you were going to the camp, laddie! Are you deaf or something, eh?'

'No, suh. Sure I's going to the camp, suh,' the driver said hurriedly.

'Like to take me along with you?'

Wolf did not wait for an answer. He opened the door and jumped into the cab.

They passed through the roadblock without the slightest difficulty. The Americans had set it up just near where the road to Weymouth passed Maiden Castle. The truck halted behind a little, boxlike pre-war English Ford, which contained, of all things, a vicar and a fat woman in a floral dress and a picture hat. The soldiers made quite a fuss of examining the two civilians' identity cards and special 'coastal area' passes, but, when it came to the truck, they cried up at the cab in bored voices, 'Dog tags and make it snappy!'

The driver made it 'snappy'. Then the soldiers saw Wolf, dressed in the uniform of a British sergeant-major and looked puzzled, as if asking themselves why a Britisher would be riding with a lot of black soldiers.

Wolf did not give them a chance to enquire too much. He opened the neck of his tunic and pulled out his identity discs. 'Here you are,' he said airily. 'Service number and all.'

The corporal, with the green leaf patch of the 4th US Infantry Division, hardly bothered to look. 'That's okay, Top,' he said and slapped the side of the cab. 'Okay, take her away.'

Half an hour later 'Sergeant-Major Hawkins' had caught a bus outside the American camp and was on his way to Weymouth.

Wolf sat in the little Salvation Army canteen, eating beans on toast and looking at the grey-painted ships which crowded the bay.

He had picked Weymouth as his target back in Berlin. There were a dozen harbours west of Portsmouth which he could have picked — Poole, Plymouth, Southampton and the like. But he chose Weymouth because it was relatively small and he had reasoned that if it were full of landing barges and transports, then the invasion fleet, limited as it was to the dozen or so harbours on that stretch of coast, would be leaving from there. Now it looked as if he had discovered what he had sought for so long — *the* stretch of coast from which they would sail. The invaders' target would be Normandy!

But Wolf knew he must make completely sure. In Berlin they had told him that the Tommies were past masters at camouflage with their dummy tanks and boats, made from rubber and three-ply. More than once they had fooled Rommel's intelligence men in the desert with their fakes. Were those boats fake too? He finished his soggy toast and left to find out.

It was a beautiful Sunday afternoon. The sun sparkled on the water. There were soldiers everywhere, strolling along the promenade, bored that there were no girls, no pubs open, nothing to do until the cinemas opened that evening, yet enjoying the sun and the sea, as if they were storing the peace for the chaos, which must soon come.

Wolf, marching proudly through them, saluting each officer he passed, British or American, with immaculate precision, as befitted a Guards sergeant-major, knew even before he reached the closest of the grey ships that these were the invaders.

The English looked mostly like recruits; they were very young and pale and skinny, the last scrapings of the barrel in a country which had about exhausted its resources after five years of war. But the Americans were different. They seemed mostly to be between 22 and 24, the best age for assault infantry; at that age a man is aggressive, unthinking, not worried about risking his life in combat. Their faces were lean and red, as if they had spent a lot of time out-of-doors, and there was an easy tough pride in their walk, a pride that comes from a lot of training and self-confidence. He noted their divisional patches too and recognized them as all coming from infantry divisions — the Fourth, the Ninth, the Seventy-Ninth. They were definitely from the assault divisions. And they were everywhere, outnumbering the shabby Tommies in their thick, new khaki serge by at least ten to one.

It took him about half an hour to reach the spot where the boats were and, when he got there, he saw that area was cordoned off. There were naval sentries armed with rifles everywhere. But the boats were real. He could see that even at that distance. Infantry barges, tank-landing craft, troop transports, he recognized them all from the identification charts they had shown him in Berlin.

'Area Z, chum. Mustn't linger around here, you know!'

Wolf turned round, startled. A red-faced Petty Officer, with the brassard of the Naval Police on his arm, was standing looking at him.

'Area Z,' Wolf said guardedly, knowing that the Hawkins tone would not go down with this man.

'If you don't know what it means, Sar'nt-Major,' the Petty Officer said, 'you don't need to know. Now I think you ought to be on your way.'

'You're probably right,' Wolf said. 'Think I'll go up to the Sally Ann.' He had heard the other soldiers use the term in the Salvation Army canteen.

'You do that,' the Petty Officer said. 'Just do that.'

Wolf marched away, but when he stooped and looked back, as he pretended to tie his boot-lace, he saw that the Petty Officer was still standing on the quay watching him. The man had obviously not believed him. He looked at his watch. It was nearly six and the first of the series of trains he would have to take to get to Swindon did not leave until ten. He could not hang around much longer in Weymouth like this. There might be someone else like the Petty Officer, who could start asking awkward questions. He must get off the streets, for a while at least.

Then he spotted her. She was standing in a doorway, smoking a cigarette, eyes half closed as the wind forced the smoke into them, her legs apart so that her thin floral dress outlined the shape of her skinny legs. As he came level with her, she took the cigarette out of her lips quite slowly and said, 'Are yer lonely, soldier?'

'What did you say?'

'Are yer looking for a good time?' she answered and her eyes sparkled with fake passion, her bright lips suddenly full of promise. She belonged to the universal order of whores like the ones he had taken so savagely on those first nights in Germany when the Bodyguard had come back from Russia to have its decimated ranks filled up once again. She was exactly what he wanted until ten o'clock.

'How much?' he asked.

'Crikey, yer quick for one of our lads,' she answered with a surprised look. 'I thought only the Yanks was that quick off the mark. Thirty bob an hour to the Americans. But for one of our lads, a quid.'

Wolf did a quick calculation. He needed money for his fare to Swindon, perhaps a couple of pounds, and he had seven left. 'How much do I get for a quid? he asked.

'An hour.'

'All right,' he said, taking out the big white five pound note. 'Will this cover me till ten?'

'Cor,' she exclaimed with genuine surprise, 'you are a glutton, aren't yer!'

'I haven't had it for a long time.'

'All right,' she said. 'My room's just around the corner.'

At nine they got out of bed and she made him a cup of tea, still clad only in her black lace bra, which for some reason she had not allowed him to take off. While she fumbled with the tea things in the little kitchen corner behind the dirty curtain, he signed the back of the five pound note for her, using Hawkins' name. 'There's a quid tip there for you,' he called and looked at the blurred photo of a young man in naval uniform on the mantelpiece. A snapshot of an American soldier was stuck in the frame.

'You oughtn't,' she called, popping her head round the curtain, 'but ta all the same.'

'Your husband, the one in naval uniform?' he asked.

'Yer. He went down with the *Hood* in 'forty-one. We'd only been married six months. The sods wasn't going to give me a pension at first.'

'I see,' Wolf said, hooking the collar of his tunic closed.

'But I'm going to get married again,' she said, emerging from the curtain with a teapot and cups on a wooden tray, 'when my Bob is finished with Area Z.'

'Area Z?'

She continued placing the tea things on the rickety table. 'Yes Area Z — Piccadilly Circus we call it in Weymouth.'

She passed him his tea. 'I can't let yer have any sugar; I used up this week's ration.'

'It's all right,' he said, then added with apparent casualness, 'What's this Area Z you were talking about?'

She looked at him over the rim of her cup. 'I thought everybody knew that down here. All this coast is part of Piccadilly Circus. It's where the boats start for the Invasion.'

At that moment Wolf could have laughed in her face. One of the most closely guarded secrets in the world this May was revealed to him casually by a pound-an-hour whore over a cup of tea. But, instead of laughing, he said, 'Nothing beats a cup of tea, does it?'

CHAPTER 4

It was the morning of the second day after the big escape. But it had obviously lost its news value for the London papers, as Taylor could see, as he looked at the front page of the *News Chronicle*. There was only a small paragraph devoted to it and the fact that the search for the 'German Air Force Lieutenant was still continuing'.

Taylor glanced at the editorial, reading again through the Churchill pledge of 21 October, 1940, in his broadcast to the French people: 'Remember we shall never stop, never weary, and never give in and that our whole people and Empire have vowed themselves to the task of cleansing Europe from the Nazi pestilence and saving the world from the new Dark Ages… Goodnight then; sleep to gather strength for the morning. For the morning will come.'

They were fine, bold, stirring words and the editor had used them to good purpose in his account of the significance of the coming Invasion. But would they come true, he asked himself. People had used the same words back in 1917 when he had been an eager young subaltern and what had happened? Now England was much more worn, more tired; the spirit somehow had gone out of the average man-in-the-street. He didn't care about victory; all he seemed to want was peace and rest.

Taylor breathed out hard and gave himself a little lecture about not letting this Wolf business get him down; it had nothing to do with him really; he just happened to be dragged into the thing. There was a knock on the door. 'Come,' he called.

Squeak limped in, munching a bacon sandwich. 'Morning,' he said, through a mouthful of bread and bacon.

'Morning!' Taylor shook his head. 'Have you not a modicum of respect for a superior officer, coming in here with your mouth full?'

Squeak grinned, 'Come off it, Bubble! Besides I was air crew and we're all deolally. Everybody knows that.'

Taylor gave a mock sigh and said, 'Anything?'

'Not a sausage. Half of Southern Command's on the lookout for him, but so far nothing. He must have gone to ground.'

Tomm looked at Taylor keenly. 'Getting you down, isn't it, Bubble?' he said.

'Yes, frankly, it is. I want to know what the bugger is up to. It must be big for them to go to all that trouble to get him into the country.'

'Agreed, but as I said yesterday on the 'phone, what use will the info be to him if he hasn't got the means of getting it out? And or him to get out of the country himself is physically impossible.'

'What if Special Branch and MI5 have *not* accounted for all the agents in this country? What if there is a sleeper somewhere, planted long ago for just this sort of thing, briefed to use his radio for just one time and transmit for Wolf? What then?'

Squeak considered for a moment. 'Okay, you might be right. They could have planted an agent way back, perhaps even before the war. But do you really think that a man — or woman — like that, who's lived here for years and has seen how things have improved since 1940 would want to stick his neck out now when we're winning? What would be in it for him?'

Taylor saw the logic of Squeak's argument. Any sleeper who sent for Wolf now would end up in the death cell at Wandsworth. But all the same he knew, however irrational it seemed under the circumstances, that Wolf must have a contact somewhere. What would have been the purpose of sending him in the first place otherwise?

'Don't worry about it, Bubble,' Squeak said. 'He'll surface again and he'll stick out like a sore thumb in that sergeant-major's uniform he nicked.'

'Maybe. Though I might remind you that there are some eight million men in uniform populating this sceptred isle at the moment.'

'Yes, but how many of them are wearing the uniform of a warrant officer, second class in the Grenadier Guards? Not many. Once he's on the move again, he'll be spotted.'

Wolf had realized by the time he caught the ten o'clock train to Dorchester, on the first stage of his journey to Swindon, that he could not wear Hawkins' uniform much longer. By now he must have discovered his loss and reported it.

At Dorchester he locked himself in the lavatories until it was time for the midnight train to Reading. When he boarded it, it was packed with soldiers, laden down with full field service marching order kit, including kitbags. In a flash all the seats in the third class vanished under the deluge of khaki with eight exhausted soldiers to a compartment, and two stretched out happily in the luggage nets, while their kit littered the corridor.

Wolf waited while the train jogged through the blacked out country side, until the soldiers began to nod off. The greatcoat was easy. There were dozens for the taking in the corridor, all neatly buttoned up and tied by the belt in the British Army fashion. He spent some time finding the right size. In the dim light of the corridor, no one saw him pick it up and slide it over his arm. Moments later he was pushing his way down the cluttered corridors to put as many coaches as possible between himself and the soldier whose coat he had stolen.

The cap was more difficult. He knew he would have to steal it from a man of the same unit, otherwise the buttons on the coat and the badge would be different and give him away.

Then again luck came his way. He was standing in another crowded corridor opposite the lavatory, when a voice behind him said, 'Excuse me, Sar'nt-Major; can I pass? I've got the trots.'

He turned. A young soldier, his face twisted with pain, stood there, holding his stomach. His tunic was ripped open, as if he could not wait to get his trousers down. His beret was thrust under his epaulette. 'On yer way, laddie,' Wolf said.

'Ta.' The young soldier pushed past him.

A little while later the man reappeared. Now he was smiling. 'Gawd, that was a load off my mind,' he said, as he squeezed by Wolf in the dimly-lit corridor.

'Yes, I'm sure it was,' Wolf said, neatly slipping the man's beret from underneath the epaulette as he passed.

At Reading station he accepted the jar of thick, dark-brown tea from the lady behind the counter of the platform YMCA canteen and took it with him into the Gents, in case there wasn't any water, which seemed to be the situation in most of the British stations. There wasn't, so he used the rest to shave with.

Locked in one of the lavatories, he used his razor blade to unpick the red flash of the Grenadier Guards from Hawkins' battledress blouse. Two light patches remained on the cloth afterwards. But that didn't worry him. He noticed that soldiers on the train had similar lighter patches where their flashes had once been. Probably it was standard operating procedure when troops were being transferred to another base, just in case the enemy was watching. He also pulled off Hawkins' brass coat-of-arms, which identified him as a warrant officer. As the London-Bristol train, which would take him to Swindon, steamed in, he reappeared on the platform as Private Sibley of the West Yorkshire Regiment.

As he pushed his way through the khaki throng heading for the exit of Swindon station, it was already morning. A warm May sun was shining on the begrimed rows of red-brick houses outside. But it was not the sun nor the houses which caught Wolf's attention. It was the two Lance-Corporals with the red caps of the Military Police standing at the exit, checking the servicemen's leave passes or the little brown books the soldiers took from their breast pockets. They were their AB 64s, Wolf knew, which all British soldiers carried. His heart sank. His identity discs would be no use here.

Swiftly he retraced his steps. Thrusting a penny in the slot machine near the barrier, he pulled out a platform ticket. Fighting his way through the crowd still coming from the London train, he brushed by the ticket collector with a hurried, 'Left me pack on the train, guv,' and flashed the platform ticket under his nose.

Desperately Wolf looked up and down the platform. Beyond lay the sprawl of the Great Western Railway's carriage works. But barring the way were two other Redcaps, advancing up the platform towards him, as if they were sheepdogs driving a herd of khaki sheep towards the pen. There was no escape in that direction. Hurriedly he turned and, dropping his platform ticket in the collector's hand, passed through the barrier again.

Wildly he sought for some way out. The crowd of soldiers at the exit was getting smaller by the second. The Redcaps would spot him at any moment. Then his gaze fell on the lavatories. He ran to the urinal, stuffing the last of his chocolate into his mouth, and scooped a handful of water from the urinal spray as the Lance-Corporal came in the door. Wolf gave a realistic groan, and bent over the bowl as if he were being sick.

The Lance-Corporal eyed him coldly. 'What's this now?' he barked harshly.

At that moment Wolf turned and let go with a choking sound. The mouthful of chewed chocolate and water spewed all about the Redcap's immaculately white-blancoed belt and across the front of his trousers. 'I'm sick!' he gasped.

'What the sodding hell do you think yer up ter?' the Redcap exploded in a paroxysm of rage. 'Look at my sodding slacks!'

Wolf looked. 'Gawd, Corp,' he breathed, 'I didn't mean to do that. Honest I didn't! But I'd been looking for the bogs ever since I got off the train. I knew I was going to toss up me guts —'

'Don't stand there like a spare prick!' the Redcap bellowed. 'Go and get something to wipe this mess off, you pig!'

'Natch, Corp. Natch!'

Wolf fled, leaving the Redcap dabbing hesitantly at the 'vomit', his face contorted with a look of disgust.

At the exit, he pushed his way boldly through the remaining soldiers to where the other Redcap was examining the brown paybooks. ''Scuse me, Corp, yer mate told me to tell yer he's having a crap. Took short like. Be back in half a mo.'

The other one didn't look up. 'Okay. Ta mate!'

Wolf passed into the May morning sunshine, hardly seeing the depressing town which Isambard Kingdom Brunel had built.

Half an hour later he was there. The briefing they had given him in Berlin had been excellent. He did not need to ask his way once in the maze of dirty, red-brick streets. He bought a copy of the *Swindon Evening Advertiser* as they had told him he must for the identification ritual, and opened it at page three. With the paper tucked under his right arm — right had been important, they had insisted in Berlin — he walked across the street to the red-brick house, which stood in its own garden not far from the church. It looked exactly as it had in the photograph that Major Ritter, alias Dr Rantzau, had taken of it in 1939 when he had done the recruitment job for the *Abwehr*, save that the windows were now criss-crossed with peeling, brown sticky tape to prevent them being shattered by blast and there was a dirty, white arrow painted on the wall near the door with the letters 'ARP SHELTER' written above it.

He rang the bell confidently, and waited, ready to say his piece: 'I read in last night's *Advertiser* — on page three — that you were looking for somebody to do the garden, sir.' It would be followed by, 'On page three, I can't recollect any such ad,' and that would be his contact.

It seemed to take the agent a long time coming. But finally he heard the shuffle of slippers coming up the passage. Slowly the heavy door creaked open. 'I read in last night's *Advertiser*,' Wolf began...

The elderly, white-haired man who stood opposite him, his face suddenly transformed from red to a deadly white, was wearing a Roman collar around his neck. The contact was a priest!

CHAPTER 5

Father Callaghan took a long time to recover himself. He was still gasping, as if he had just suffered a heart attack, and the bony hand which held the whisky still trembled. He needed both hands when he raised the glass to his lips. Wolf waited. It was good to sit down after two days without sleep. Let the priest take his time to recover. But there was a nagging doubt that all was not well. What had he meant with those first shocked words, 'But why me — *now?*'

He studied the priest, whose face had returned to the beetroot red of those who suffer from high blood pressure. Somehow he disliked the man. He looked too gross, too well-fed to be a man of God, rather like those arrogant, pot gut priests they had once used to caricature in the old *Simplicissimus*. And there was something in the man's eyes, which even his present fear could not quite hide — a certain disturbing un-Christian cunning. He shrugged and told himself he was imagining things. Schellenberg had spoken most highly of the man. And, besides, with the kind of work he had been doing these last years, the priest would have to be cunning.

Finally he put down his glass and asked in a soft Irish voice, not quite under control, 'But why did they send you to me, my son?'

'Because you are our only agent in this part of the country, Father. Berlin spoke most highly of you. Besides, you have the *AFU* transmitter.'

Callaghan looked at him in complete bewilderment. 'But who told you that?'

Wolf looked back at him, equally bewildered. This was not the usual security pose agents adopted with each other at the beginning; this was something else. 'General Schellenberg told me. I don't understand.'

'I don't either, my son,' the priest said. 'I haven't had the *AFU* since I was blown in 1942.'

'Blown?'

'Yes, uncovered?'

'By the British?'

'No.' The Priest shook his snow-white head slowly. 'Your people.'

'But,' Wolf gasped. 'I don't understand.'

Then the Reverend Patrick Callaghan, once known to the Twenty Committee as *Beetroot*, told him.

In 1922, when Michael Collins had been gunned down, the 'Boys' had advised Callaghan that it would be better if he went to England — 'and yesterday'd be better than today, Father,' they had said. So he had first come to England, the country he had been taught all his life to hate.

To his surprise, the English were not so bad after all, some of them indeed were quite kind. At Liverpool, always sympathetic to the Irish, the Archbishop had not asked too many questions as to why a young priest should abandon his parish without leave from his Bishop. Instead he had given him a job looking after one of the Catholic seamen's missions. He had stayed there for a couple of years until he had been given a curacy at St Wilfred's, York, under old Canon Chadwick. Again his people had been mainly Irish or descendants of those who had fled the potato famine. In 1930 he had been given his own parish, on the fringes of Swindon, looking after the Catholic railwaymen whose ancestors had come to the town as 'navigators' to build the great complex at the junction of the Great Western's main lines to Bristol, Bath, South Wales and Cheltenham. Brunel and Daniel Gooch had made provision for nearly everything at Swindon — schools, medical centre, Protestant churches. But they had forgotten the Catholic 'navvies'. They were forced to erect their own little church on the outskirts of town and it was there that Father Callaghan had come in 1930.

In 1935 his mother had died. He had gone home to the funeral, naturally. In the village they still observed the 'wake' and this one had gone on for three long days, filled with an endless round of porter and poteen, tears and tales, hymns of praise and hymns of hate, and suddenly, without his hardly knowing it, the 'Boys' had him again.

But this time it was different. At first he hadn't realized who their real masters were. But in early 1939, when the letter-box campaign was at its height and he was hiding up to forty pounds of TNT at a time behind the altar in the church for them, he had received a strange visitor. The man spoke English with an American accent, but Callaghan had spotted immediately that he was neither American nor English. His clothes and his extreme politeness (at the beginning at least) had given him away — he was German.

The man got down to business at once. 'Father,' he said, 'we all know and respect your contribution to the cause.'

'What cause?'

The German smiled very politely and said, 'You don't need to know more than that I am Rantzau. But I'll tell you this. My organization has worked with yours before. Remember Casement?'

The penny dropped. 'You're from German Intelligence?' Rantzau simply overheard the question. 'Soon, Father, there will be a new war and Ireland will be on Germany's side. Their causes will be the same — the defeat and downfall of Britain. If you help us, you will be helping Ireland to free herself from the British yoke.'

'And if I don't?'

Rantzau smiled and said nothing.

Two weeks before the outbreak of war, in the August of 1939, he had received another German visitor, this time from the Embassy in London, who brought him the *AFU* set in a brown leather case and spent a week showing him how to use it. Thereafter there had followed two years of nights spent down by the station observing the movements of troops and goods heading for Bristol and the Atlantic run and passing the information on to Hamburg by radio to be used for guiding Dönitz's U-boat wolf packs.

In the end, the English came for him one Sunday morning in June, 1941. There were three of them, in felt hats and heavy macs. They had been very polite, softly-spoken and utterly confident they had the right man, in spite of his protestations that he didn't know what they were talking about.

Later he found out why, in London. One of the 'Boys' had talked for money — too much drink or too much money, it's Ireland's curse, his mother had always said. And so with visions of a long prison sentence and perhaps even worse looming in his mind, he had broken down and confessed.

They remained very polite, the 'gentlemen' from London, as he called them, for they never introduced themselves. They were ready to 'make a certain proposition' to him. It was that he should work for them, continuing to use the *AFU* for certain messages which they thought useful. Would he agree to be 'turned', as they put it?

He asked what the alternative was and the older one, who looked like a university professor (which he was), said very casually, 'Oh, well, I suppose the Landlord wouldn't mind hanging a clergyman.'

Later he found out that they were referring to a man who kept a pub and did their hangings for them.

He shuddered and agreed. Thus, by the end of 1941 he was in touch with Hamburg again, but this time he was working under the control of British Intelligence. The Twenty Committee had him firmly under its heavy thumb.

But the 'game', as they called it, didn't last more than nine months. In early 1942, after the British had sunk five U-boats in the Atlantic as a result of information he had passed on, Ritter — for that was Rantzau's real name — had advised his chief, Admiral Canaris, that something was wrong.

'I think it's obvious, sir. *Tomato* has been turned by the Tommies.'

And that had been the end of *Beetroot's*, alias *Tomato's*, career with the two Intelligence services. Twenty Committee had been 'rather nice' about it, as Masterman had put it. He was to be allowed to stay with his parish as long as he had nothing more to do with the 'Boys' and naturally, with the 'opposition'. His career as a double-agent was over.

Wolf looked at the fat priest in confused amazement. 'But if they knew that you were blown,' he gasped, 'why did they send me here?'

It took Callaghan a long time to answer. Outside in the hall the grandfather clock ticked away the moments of their life with grim inexorability. Finally he said, 'My son, I don't know. But in these last years I have learned a lot about them.'

Wolf knew at once whom he meant by 'them'.

'And I have discovered they are very devious people who don't let their left hand know what their right hand is doing.' For the first time since Wolf had entered that house, he looked him straight into the eyes. 'My son, I believe that some horrible wickedness has been done to you.'

CHAPTER 6

'Can I do you now, sir?' Squeak said, in a fair imitation of Mrs Mopp's voice.

Taylor woke with a startled grunt. It had been a long warm May afternoon and the routine boring paperwork on his desk, added to the three double whiskies he had had instead of lunch, had lulled him into an uneasy sleep.

'What is it?'

Squeak beamed down at him joyously. 'They've got the bugger.'

'Squeak, for someone with a First, your ability to express yourself clearly is about nil. Who has got what bugger?'

Squeak's smile didn't vanish. 'Just got a tinkle from Masterman at Twenty. They've bagged Wolf.'

'What?'

'Yes, apparently he turned up this morning at one of their agents. That vicar chap down in the West Country — the one who was burnt donkey's years ago. Being the soul of Christian kindness, the good vicar turned him in to the local gendarmes as soon as Wolf's back was turned.'

'So there *was* something more to Wolf all the time?'

'Looks like it, doesn't it. Anyway they want you to go down on the night train with the Special Branch chap and Gaines of Twenty Committee. You're to identify him for them.'

Taylor was only half-listening. 'But why go to all the trouble to dump him into the lap of someone they knew was blown all the time?' he asked of no one in particular.

Tomm shrugged easily. 'To coin a cliché, it's a funny old world. Now, you'd better get your skates on if you're going to catch that train to Swindon.'

Paddington Station was crowded. There were troops everywhere. Half the regiments in the British Army seemed to be represented there and the loudspeakers over the RTO's office kept booming out names of units and trains every few seconds. Officious NCOs with the red brassard of the RTO on their arms pushed through the throng, checking names and units on their clipboards. Hard-eyed Redcaps were posted at every corner and every exit.

The three of them, Taylor, Gaines and the stony-faced Detective Sergeant from Special Branch stood to one side, to allow a battalion of Coldstream Guards to march by.

'They're putting them in the cages,' the Sergeant said.

'Cages?' Taylor asked.

'Sealing them up for the Invasion, Sir. It can't be long now.' They pushed their way through the throng to the first class carriage which had been reserved for them.

The fat Priest was obviously drunk when he opened the door to them. Taylor could smell the whisky on his breath and wished he could be drunk too. There was something nasty about a Priest who betrayed a fugitive to the Police. But then, he knew from Gaines, the Priest had had enough experience of betraying people right back to the days of Michael Collins.

He ushered them into his study and they got down to business at once. Taylor let Gaines and the Special Branch man have their turn first. The man babbled on, his tongue loosened by the whisky and his relief that he had got out of the nasty affair so easily.

Finally Gaines looked at his watch. It was midnight. He turned to Taylor. 'Do you want to ask him anything before we go over to the jail?'

'Yes, I would.' He turned to the Priest. 'What was his reaction when you told Wolf you hadn't been working for the Germans for over two years?' He omitted the 'Father'. Somehow it seemed indecent to use the title with someone who had waited until a fugitive dropped off before sneaking to the nearest phone to betray him.

'Absolute incredulity,' Callaghan said. 'He just wouldn't believe me. He thought I was afraid that he was some sort of *agent provocateur* like the Tans used,' he bit his lip as he realized that he'd made a bloody foolish slip — 'who was trying to compromise me. He said that he had information of supreme importance for the German cause and I *must* help him.'

'Was it about the area of coast from which we intend to launch the Invasion?' Taylor asked.

'That's right. He had deduced it from the amount and type of shipping at Weymouth.'

'With what he knows he is heading straight for the cooler until the landings are over,' Gaines said to himself.

Taylor hesitated. So his guess at Monty's HQ had been right! That was what Wolf had been after all along. But still there was the mystery of why Berlin had directed him right into the arms of this particular Irish Judas.

'Is that all?' he said.

'No. When I insisted that I was not their man any longer, he seemed to crack up. To me he had appeared such a strong man, although very tired. But suddenly it all appeared to be too much for him. It was like sometimes in the confessional when they tell me their secrets and they're sad and glad at the same time, sobbing and protesting. But he got a grip of himself after a while and had another crack at me, as if he still didn't believe what I had said. He told me how his chief, a general named Schellenheim or something like that…'

'Schellenberg,' Gaines corrected him and looked significantly at Taylor.

'That could have been the name,' the Priest continued. 'But at all events this General had to know the site of the Invasion because they have some sort of mobile weapon — rockets…'

Taylor interrupted. 'Let's have that again,' he said, leaning forward.

The Priest swallowed. 'There was this German assault engineer regiment — Number Fifty it was — that I remember distinctly. That was its cover, because its real purpose was to fire some sort of rocket weapon off the back of lorries.'

'You are sure the number was Fifty?'

'Certain.'

Taylor stood up suddenly. 'Sergeant, will you take Reverend Callaghan outside for a moment? Something very important had come up, which is not for his ears.'

Taylor waited until the two of them had left the room. Then he told Gaines about Wachtel and his *Flakregiment*. 'Now, Wachtel surfaced yesterday after this mysterious vanishing act just where we anticipated he would reappear — in the area of the new sites on the Channel coast along the *Pas de Calais*. We had thought that he and his officers had gone underground while the Jerries were building up a new line of less detectable sites after we'd knocked out most of the old line during the winter. But this puts a new complexion on the whole matter. It could mean that they have been able to set up a second regiment with some sort of mobile weapon and that Wachtel's disappearance had something to do with it. Now he has returned to his old regiment, the 155th, to make us believe that we've got the missile situation tabbed, while there is this gash one floating around to let us have it on the day.'

'What day?'

'D-Day.' Taylor answered simply. 'At present the Jerries' bases are all directed to fire at London and the Southampton-Portsmouth area. We worked that out last year when we started bombing them. From that we could work out the Jerries' strategy.'

'To terrorize the capital and perhaps knock out the probable embarkation ports for an attack on either of the two key sectors, *Pas de Calais* or Normandy?'

'Right. But imagine what would happen on the day, if a new mobile unit suddenly popped up from nowhere and started plastering the beaches? A unit which could reach either beach, assuming that the Jerries were still confused about our intended landing site, within a matter of hours?'

Gaines looked at him aghast. 'It'd be a massacre!'

Taylor nodded.

'But what are we going to do about it?'

'Not *we* — I.' He took hold of Gaines' arm and guided him gently to the door. 'I'm afraid that I'm going to have to ask you to leave. I'm going to talk to someone whose name and occupation I cannot reveal even to you.'

Gaines nodded. 'I understand.' he said, although in truth he didn't. Twenty Committee surely knew all the secret organizations in the country! 'What about Wolf?' he asked as Taylor began to close the door on him.

'We'll attend to him in the morning. He is no longer of any importance.'

He closed the door and listened as Gaines walked down the corridor to the others. Then he picked up the 'phone. 'Trunks,' he said and gave the girl the well-known London number.

CHAPTER 7

For an officer of his rank, Taylor was a man who knew more than his ration of the country's top secrets. He had become aware of the Double-Cross System and Twenty Committee's work almost as soon as it had been set up in early 1941. He had become a 'Bigot', one of the few men of his rank in the whole of the Allied armies who was so honoured, a week after the Cossack Plan had been approved at Quebec in 1943 and the date set. But it wasn't until January, 1944, that the Prime Minister himself had approved his initiation into the secrets of Bletchley and the activities of Winterbotham's 'Shadow OKW' and he had become an 'Ultra'.

Naturally Winterbotham hadn't told him everything, for although he was officially in the RAF his real loyalty was to the Secret Intelligence Service; and the SIS boys, Taylor knew of old, only told you what you needed to know — and no more. But what little the SIS man had told him had been startling enough — that the secret wireless station at Bletchley had been able to crack all the main German secret codes, used by the *Abwehr*, Army, Navy and Air Force since May, 1940. By the spring of 1941 they had been in a position to work out not only the whole German order-of-battle, down sometimes to battalion or even company level, but also the enemy's operational intentions, sometimes even before the lower-ranking German recipients of the operational orders were aware of what was coming their way.

In 1942, so Winterbotham explained, the operation had been taken a stage further and what the Bletchley boffins called 'the Shadow *OKW*' set up. This organization, the British version of the real German *OKW*, or *Oberkommando der Wehrmacht*, had tried to organize the huge mass of information that was coming into Bletchley into some manageable form, attempting to think as the real German High Command would, so that it could be fielded out to certain specific Army Commanders for their information. Now Winterbotham was head of the security organization which guarded the treasured secrets passed out to a handful of key generals.

It was the Chief of Ultra security whom Taylor now called, with his first request of that long May night.

His next call — Winterbotham had woken up and responded to his query with surprising good humour for a man who liked his sleep — was to Jones.

Jones, of Scientific Air Intelligence, was still awake and as lively as ever in spite of the lateness of the hours. 'Hello Professor,' he said 'and to what do I owe the honour?'

Taylor told him.

Jones was deadly serious now. 'I see,' he snapped. 'That would create a very grave situation indeed. Let me have a think about it — and consult the oracle.'

The 'Oracle' was a mysterious list of top-secret German war projects which had been thrust through the letter box of the British Embassy in Oslo in late 1939. Nobody knew where it had come from and nobody had quite believed it at the time. It had contained references to something called 'heavy water' and an 'atomic bomb' and rocket missiles and the like. But Jones had, and over the years the unknown German scientist who had supplied them in this strange way with the details of all current top-secret German research had been proved right time and time again.

His third call was to Duncan Sandys. But his duty officer had replied in a bored, tired, upper-class drawl that his 'master' was dining at Number Ten. He left a message with the man to inform his 'master' at once what had developed in the missile war, in which the British side was commanded by Sandys, and hung up.

Jones rang back at about three o'clock.

'Well, Doctor?' Taylor demanded.

'The Oracle says no. Back in 1939, at least, the Germans had no plans for making them mobile. At that time they were hoping for a rather accurate type of missile, the fire of which could be pin-pointed. After all Dornberger, or whatever the chap who's in charge at Peenemunde is called, is an artillery man and you know the devotees of Saint Barbara — they're very hot on accuracy. Since then they have taken nearly four years to develop a missile which has less than a kilometre deviation in a flight range of — say — two hundred and fifty kilometres. And they have only been able to achieve that kind of accuracy from fixed sites. So, for my money, the mobile missile is not yet on. After all it was only when Speer could convince Hitler on Christmas Eve, 1942 — and my God, what a time to pick — that the V-1 had less than a kilometre deviation that he allowed the thing to go into mass production.'

'So that's your considered opinion — no mobile missile?'

'It definitely is,' Jones answered without hesitation.

'Goodnight, Doctor, and thanks.'

Winterbotham startled him out of an uneasy sleep in which he dreamed that rockets were falling by the score on a beach which bore a strong resemblance to Clacton-on-Sea. It was five o'clock.

'Wild goose-chase,' Winterbotham said. 'The boffins at the Shadow *OKW* went through their total order of battle on both the west and east fronts, just in case.'

'And?'

'No 50th Assault Engineers. They simply don't exist,'

'What do you make of it?'

'Couldn't rightly say — unless it's a come-on.'

'What do you mean?'

'Well, of course, I don't know. It's not my department. But this 50th Assault Engineer thing could be a plant.'

'A plant! But why?'

'Couldn't say. But I'll give you a bit of buckshee info on the side. I got it on the QT from Menzies.' Colonel Menzies was head of the Secret Intelligence Service. 'Schellenberg, the chap you mentioned, who sent this agent into the UK in the first place. Well, he's been making noises since last autumn which sound suspiciously like those of a dove.'

'You mean peace overtures?'

'I certainly do.'

'But he's in the SS. Why should he do anything like that?'

'Search me, old chap,' Winterbotham answered wearily. 'I'm beat and I've got an early morning conference with Patton tomorrow.' And with that, Wing Commander Winterbotham hung up, leaving Taylor completely bewildered.

There was only one more call that night — one that came from a totally unexpected source, just after six o'clock. It was Swindon Main Police Station, reporting that the prisoner Wolf had just escaped.

BOOK FOUR: *THE PLAN — LA ROCHE-GUYON, FRANCE (JANUARY, 1944)*

'Hundred and fifty days to go'

CHAPTER 1

For *Brigadeführer* Walter Schellenberg, the series of events which had led to Operation Cuckoo's Egg, as he called it, had begun one hot August day at the *Reichsführer* SS's HQ at Vinnitsa in the occupied Ukraine. To be exact, 23 August, 1942. The mood at Himmler's HQ was depressed. The summer offensive in Southern Russia and that in Egypt were obviously running into serious difficulties, and Schellenberg, though no soldier, knew that if the German armies failed to break through in the Caucasus and in Egypt, the die was cast. Germany had lost her gamble for world power. The time had come to end the war.

An elegant, penniless ex-lawyer, Schellenberg had come a long way since he first joined the SS, but he had never been blinded by the lies of the '1,000 Year Reich'. He was not prepared, as he told his second wife, 'to lay at the feet of the totalitarian state the tribute of his loyalty unto death'. He wanted to survive the war, whoever won, and continue his life in the same luxurious style as he led it now. He was not going to participate in the *Gotterdammerung* of the Third Reich if he could help it.

Thus that blazing hot afternoon he faced the head of the SS and said straight out, '*Reichsführer*, in which drawer of your desk do you keep your alternative solution for ending the war?'

Himmler's pale face flushed and he looked up at his young subordinate in rage and bewilderment. 'Have you gone mad?' he cried. 'Are you losing your nerve?'

Schellenberg's expression did not change. '*Reichsführer*,' he answered, 'I knew you'd go on like this.' He smiled a little. 'In fact I thought it might be worse.'

For a while Himmler continued in his most angry manner, but gradually he began to calm down. He knew and respected Schellenberg, 'my Benjamin' as he called him, the man who had once saved him from death in an aeroplane and who, although he was very ambitious, was not after his own job as *Reichsführer*, as so many of the younger men in the Reich Main Security Office were. 'But what can we do?' he asked after a while, wiping the sweat from his forehead.

Schellenberg had his answer ready; after all he had been thinking for quite a while now about what had to be done. 'There is tension between the Western Allies and the Russians, as everyone knows.'

Himmler nodded. Now the Russians were beginning to win their war, there were many in important positions in the West, both British and Americans, who were starting to remember their old fears of Soviet Russia. Agent reports from the neutral capitals were full of details about Allied diplomats' and businessmen's concern about the 'Red Bogeyman'.

'Accordingly, while still continuing our struggle against the Reds, *Reichsführer*, we must begin secret peace discussions with the Western Allies. We must find out what their terms will be for such an undertaking.'

Reichsführer Himmler, 'Loyal Heinrich', had given his approval. Thus the business had started.

It had not been easy. The British distrusted Schellenberg — he knew that well. After all he had been the brain behind the luring and kidnapping of Britain's two key spymasters over the Dutch-German border at the beginning of the war. Then, too, he had used the dodge that he represented the 'resistance' against Hitler. In London, they feared, understandably, that he was attempting to pull the same trick once again. So he ordered his agents to approach the Americans first.

The man they picked was described in the SD files as 'a tall, burly, sporting type of about 45, healthy-looking with good teeth and a fresh simple open-hearted manner'. With the Swiss Cantonal Police the American who lived at Number 23 Herrengasse, Berne, was registered as Mr Bull and he had something vaguely to do with the American Embassy. In fact, his real name was Allen W. Dulles, the European head of the OSS and according to the SD files 'the most influential White House man in Europe'.

Mr Bull's manner was indeed 'open-hearted'. At his first meeting with Schellenberg's two representatives he told them that while America might be prepared to negotiate, there was one essential pre-condition: 'Hitler must go.' Thereupon he had retreated behind his pipe, beaming at their shocked faces, and said no more on the subject. But it was quite obvious how he thought the Führer should 'go'.

Himmler was horrified when Schellenberg reported on the meeting.

'Never!' he cried, banging his fist on the table, 'I, the head of the Führer's own SS, cannot have the greatest brain in Europe assassinated!'

But Schellenberg had persisted. He contacted the Americans in Spain this time and discussed with them his 'Operation KN' — KN for Kidnap. On paper at least, he had already worked out a foolproof plan to kidnap Hitler with his own SD experts, trained at Hunting Commando's remote country lodge. They would fly the kidnapped Leader immediately out of the country in his own four-engined Condor to Spain. After landing, the

Führer would be taken by fast car to the port of Valencia, where he would be smuggled past the Spanish authorities in a small tramp steamer already rented for the purpose. From there the ship would sail along the Spanish coast to Gibraltar, where he would be handed over to the Allied authorities to do with him as they pleased. Immediately it was announced that the Führer had disappeared — and it was calculated that the whole operation, from the kidnapping to the landing at Gibraltar, would not take more than forty-eight hours — Himmler would take over the leadership of Germany and begin negotiations with the Western Allies. 'Loyal Heinrich' would not raise his own hand against the 'greatest brain in Europe', but he had no objection to the Allies doing it.

But the great plan was not destined to go into operation. Even Schellenberg's SD men could not find a way of getting through the new security screen thrown around the Führer at his various HQs, which had grown from a handful of men of the Bodyguard in 1939 to a 100-strong *Begleitkommando* and nearly a regiment of picked troops, including anti-aircraft gunners, by 1943.

1943 had given way to 1944 without any further progress in the attempt to dispense with the burden of Adolf Hitler, the only way out if the Western Allies were going to make peace with Germany before it was too late.

Now it was obvious — even to Himmler — that Germany had virtually lost the war in the East and soon she would be fighting for her very existence in the West. 'Once the Western Allies land in France, *Reichsführer*', Schellenberg drummed home the warning time and time again, 'it will be only a matter of months, perhaps even weeks, before we're finished. It will have to be unconditional surrender, as they are now demanding, and the end of your SS dream.'

'The SS dream' of a Germanic Europe, run by his own blond, blue-eyed SS warriors, was, Schellenberg knew, the darling of the *Reichsführer's* romantic, sentimental and completely absurd heart. It meant more to him than his loyalty to Hitler.

'But what are we to do?' he had moaned and wrung his soft, pale hands, whenever Schellenberg brought up the subject. 'I can't have my SS kill the Führer. Besides they would never do it.'

But there Himmler was wrong.

By the start of 1944, the elite of the Armed SS was stationed in France, awaiting the invasion. They were not the rabble of Ukrainians, Turkomen, Croatians, Latvians and a dozen other Eastern nations, who by no stretch of the imagination could be called 'Germanic' and 'Aryan'. These were the *German* SS Divisions. The *Bodyguard*, the *Hitler Youth* the *Death's Head*, the SS *Imperial Guards* — and they were no longer prepared to be sacrificed in Normandy or the *Pas de Calais* like the Great Emperor's Imperial Guard had been at Waterloo. They had all been through the murderous Russian battles and were heartily sick of the terrible losses they had suffered there.

But the commanders of the six divisions, formed into the 1st and 2nd SS Panzer Corps, lacked a leader and a plan for putting an end to the war before it was too late for the Reich, That is until *Obergruppenführer* Wilhelm Bittrich, commander of 2nd SS Panzer Corps, had his first serious talk with the commander of the land forces in France, the 'Desert Fox'. Field Marshal Rommel was now a different man from the Rommel who had gone to Africa in 1941. Hitler had awarded him great honours for his leadership of the *Afrika Korps* and Rommel had been convinced of the Leader's greatness. But by early 1944 the 'Desert Fox' knew that Hitler must go. As he told his Chief of Staff, General Speidel, 'We must ensure the arrest of Adolf Hitler and his arraignment before a German court.' Rommel envisaged a two-fold strategy: Hitler would be arrested, and when that was done, all the German troops in the Occupied Territories in the West would withdraw behind the Siegfried Line, letting the Allies land and take over at their leisure. Then Germany would sue for peace with her armies intact.

During that first talk with the sharp-featured SS General, who was known throughout the Armed SS for his acid tongue, Rommel sounded him out on what the Imperial Guard's reaction to any such move would be. Bittrich pulled no punches: 'My knowledge is not restricted to this front, Field Marshal. I know how bad things are on the Eastern front too. There is no more objective leadership there. All that's happening is a lot of crude tricks to keep our heads above water. Up there they don't realize the danger because they're completely out of touch. I'm not going to carry out senseless orders and have my young men slaughtered for damn all.'

Then Rommel told him of his own plan.

The SS General clicked his polished riding boots together and snapped, 'Field Marshal, I am with you and so is the Second SS Panzer Corps. My commanders think exactly as I do.'

Thus the Imperial Guard joined in the plot to 'eradicate' their one-time master. Under Rommel's command the whole of the Occupation Forces would march back to Germany and take up their positions on Germany's frontiers, leaving the West wide open for the invading Allied armies. But there was one catch. *How were they going to arrest Hitler?*

It was here that *Brigadeführer* Schellenberg, who had his spies everywhere, had come to their assistance. For a very long time Schellenberg had known of the *Wehrmacht's* plan to get rid of Hitler. But none of their assassination and kidnapping schemes had been able to overcome the basic problem: how to get through Hitler's protective screen. As Schellenberg had told a small, intimate conference of the senior SS Generals and Army Generals in the plot, 'So many agencies within the Reich would have to come under the control of the plotters at once so that, immediately after the assassination, they would be able to reassure the great mass of the civilian population and the Army that everything was in their hands, they were the new and legitimate government. In other words, gentlemen, one needs a place for the attempt, which is beyond the normal security precautions and which is fully under the control of the plotters. He had let his words sink in and then said, 'I think I have such a place for you.'

CHAPTER 2

'*The Valley of the Wolf, Number Two*, Field Marshal,' he had answered Rommel's query.

'The Führer's Headquarters in France,' General Dietrich, the Commander of the 1st SS Panzer Corps, exclaimed. 'At Margival? But how can you know *now*, so far ahead, that the Führer is going to come to France? In the old days of the Bodyguard, I had to take care of the security arrangements for the Führer myself. I know how he always insisted that people should only know at the last possible minute what his agenda was for any particular day.'

'I agree with you, General,' Schellenberg said smoothly, realizing how far the rot had set in if an old Party bully-boy like Dietrich, who had been one of the first organizers of the SS, were prepared to plot against Hitler. 'But this time it is different. The Führer is coming to France to supervise the start of the V-1 campaign against London, which he fondly — and I think unrealistically — hopes will bring the Tommies to their knees.

'I understand. And you know, of course, the date when the V-1 campaign will start?'

'Right.' Schellenberg pointed to the big map of Northern France on the wall behind him at Rommel's HQ, where he was holding the briefing. 'The Führer will arrive at Metz airport in his usual Condor. From there he will take the Mercedes. Kempka will be waiting for him with the car at Metz. In all likelihood they'll drive along the main Verdun-Reims road to Soissons before turning off for the Valley of the Wolf at Margival along the D 537.'

He let them absorb the information for a minute, then continued: 'Now somewhere along that route, *Hauptsturmführer* Schulze, head of the SS Escort, will alert your headquarters at La Roche-Guyon, *Herr Generalfeldmarschal*, that the Führer is on his way and that you are to attend him at the Valley of the Wolf.'

Rommel nodded. That was the usual way Hitler did such things to prevent himself being shot at by some would be assassin.

'Then Schulze will alert local security. In the Condor, the Führer will be unable to take more than his personal body guard with him, so he'll need more men to carry out the normal drill.'

'Yes, that's true,' Dietrich agreed thoughtfully. 'Then where is he going to get the men from to carry out the usual surveillance duties?'

'Well, General, one thing is certain, he will not ask the local army units for assistance. Schulze won't trust them. If you'll forgive me, Field Marshal,' Schellenberg looked at Rommel, 'in the Reich Main Security Office we have little faith in the Army's reliability any more.'

Rommel did not react. He accepted the information as a fact of life. 'All right, *Brigadeführer* where will this man Schulze ask for the troops he requires to seal off the Margival area?'

Schellenberg flung out his well-manicured hand at the SS Generals. 'There, Field Marshal, from his most loyal men, the Armed SS.'

Dietrich frowned a little at the words, but the others' facial expressions didn't change, although Schellenberg was implying that they were the worst kind of traitors.

'He will ask the nearest SS division for, say, a battalion to do the job.' He looked at the gigantic figure of General Witt, the commander of the *Hitler Youth*, the average age of whose soldiers was 19. 'Your division, I think, General, if my memory serves me right.'

'It does.' Witt had joined the conspiracy because he could not visualize sending his young hopefuls, virtually every one of them a volunteer from the *Hitler Youth*, to be slaughtered against hopeless odds. Now he asked, 'And what would my task be?'

Schellenberg hesitated. He knew quite well that Himmler, his master, now conversant with his daring plan, would never tolerate Hitler being arraigned before a German court as Rommel had proposed. The *Reichsführer* must finally be taught the facts of life — he must be made brave whether he wanted to be or not. There was only one way left to deal with Adolf Hitler. 'Your task? It would be quite simple. *It would be to kill the Führer!*'

He waited until the excited clamour had died down, he had time. After all, he had been waiting for nearly two years to put his own 'final solution' into practice which would make him Himmler's Grey Eminence and the number two man in the post-war German state.

'But don't you see the beauty of the plan? There will be no Görings, no Bormanns, no Gestapo Müllers, no Keitels, no Jodls to get in our way. Hitler will be completely at our mercy, cut off from his normal channels to the outer world. Let us say he is planning at that time to spend at least twenty-four hours in France to watch the progress of the V-1 offensive; with luck perhaps even thirty-six. After all, he has been promising the nation for months now that the revenge weapons will break the back of the English and pay them back for what their own air terrorists have done to Germany since 1942. It is a highly important event in the Führer's life.'

Several of the SS Generals nodded their agreement.

'So, for twenty-four hours we will have Germany in the palm of our hands.' He bent his hand upwards, palm crooked, fingers turned in on each other. 'No one is asking questions. No one is getting in our way. Almost as if the Führer were spending a weekend with his paramour.'

One or two of his listeners laughed. By now all of them knew that the 'great ascetic', as he had once called himself, married 'only to the nation', had taken to himself a mistress, Eva Braun.

'And in that time, gentlemen, the Army will have taken over complete control in the East and in the West, and the *Reichsführer SS* within the Reich. Twenty-four hours after the Führer's — er — sudden heart attack Himmler will take over the reins as the Führer's successor. The last will and testament is ready — forged naturally.' He smiled at them. 'And the German Army in the West under the command of Field Marshal Rommel, will be moving back to the Reich'.

Schellenberg stopped and let them digest the sheer audacity of the plan for a few moments, his eyes flashing from face to face, taking in each individual General's reaction, willing each one of them to approve.

And, one by one, he could see they were approving — Rommel, Speidel, Dietrich, Witt, Harzig and all the rest of them. All save one, *Generalleutnant* Bittrich. His face, above the gleaming black and white bauble of the Knight's Cross of the Iron Cross, was cold and still unconvinced, though Schellenberg knew from his own agents on the General's staff that he was against any continuation of the war.

'You are pulling a rather stuffy face, General?' he queried, knowing that he could not go back now.

'Yes,' Bittrich said.

'You are not convinced?'

'No, not that,' Bittrich answered. 'But I have a question, the answer to which I think is vital to the success of any undertaking such as you have just outlined.'

Schellenberg bowed slightly.

'When is the Führer to visit France for the start of the V-1 campaign against England?'

'On the seventeenth of June, 1944.'

Bittrich threw up his hands in despair. 'My God, Schellenberg, the seventeenth of June! Do you still believe in Santa Claus?'

'What do you mean, Herr Bittrich?'

'I mean, do you really think that the Tommies and the *Amis* will wait *that* long before they invade France? At 2nd Panzer Corps we expect them in May when the weather is usually pretty good in this part of the world.'

'And let me point out,' Rommel said, 'that our estimate is that with the forces available to us in France, the German Army will only be able to hold off the Anglo-Americans for — say — three weeks. Don't you agree, Speidel?'

Speidel nodded. 'If we are lucky,' he said.

Schellenberg smiled back at them soothingly, as if they were a rebellious class of schoolboys who had just been told they were to lose one of their holidays. 'Gentlemen, gentlemen,' he said, holding up his hands. 'Don't you think we have not thought of that problem? After all, we in Intelligence know more of such things than you do. We have our agents everywhere in England.' It was a lie, but a necessary one to calm them down. 'We know well when the Anglo-Americans will invade.'

'I should be grateful if you would just tell me *where* they will invade,' Rommel said icily.

'Have no fear. If you will bear me out for a moment, Field-Marshal, you will see that the problem of *where* they will invade is no longer of this much importance. For by that time, the German Army will probably already have evacuated France. The Anglo-Americans will be able to land where and how they please, without a shot being fired. We might even leave a little money behind for the French so that they send down a bunch of patriotically inclined school-children to wave the Stars and Stripes and the Union Jack at them as they wade ashore.'

'Oh, for God's sake!' Bittrich snapped.

Schellenberg wasn't disturbed. He had the measure of these men. Times were changing. The day would come when men like Bittrich wouldn't dare to question him if they valued their lives. 'Very well, gentlemen, in Berlin we have worked out a plan, which we feel will make the Tommies and their *Ami* friends postpone their invasion till the latter of the two anticipated good weather periods in the Channel, which are, according to the experts I have consulted, traditionally in early May and late June.'

Rommel nodded.

'So,' Schellenberg continued, 'my own secret weather stations in Spitzbergen and the Azores would then be able to forecast *exactly* on the basis of the weather conditions over Novia Scotia and Newfoundland and over the Azores when in the last few days of June they would come.'

Rommel looked up at him coldly. 'Secret weather stations in Spitzbergen and the Azores, a plan to make them postpone the invasion. My mind reels, Schellenberg! What is all this?'

Schellenberg knew he had them now. With deceptive modesty, he said: 'My Hunting Commando, *Herr Generalfeldmarschal.*'

CHAPTER 3

'The Hunting Commando, gentlemen, was formed to carry out operations of a more violent and aggressive nature than those executed by the traditional secret service operative. Less brain, shall we say, and more muscle. The rescue of Mussolini from the Gran Sasso last year by Skorzeny is typical of the Hunting Commando's operations. After all Skorzeny is its head.'

Schellenberg saw the look of alarm that flashed across their . faces at the mention of the Austrian's name and said, 'Of course, Skorzeny knows nothing of this operation. The man is still devoted to his Führer. A community of blood, perhaps, between two Austrians. I don't know. But, to return to the matter in hand, the members of Hunting Commando come from every nation in Europe — we even have one Jew, I believe. Whatever their motives for joining, they are all bold, resourceful men, who speak the language of the country in which they operate. For your information, we have at this present time two operatives and a woman from the Commando working in Moscow. Our frogmen have tapped the Atlantic cable so that we can listen to Churchill and Roosevelt conversing, though we are having some difficulty at the *Reichspost* about unscrambling the speech when they use the scrambler. We have a man on the Seydlitz Committee and at least three operatives in the Generals' camps in Russia, where we suppose there will be a number of defectors. We have other agents preparing to seize the Citadel of Budapest, if Horthy, the Hungarian dictator, goes any further in his secret peace talks with the Russians…'

Schellenberg rattled off the names and places with the confidence of an expert conjuror producing rabbit after rabbit from his top hat. 'This, then,' he concluded his little *tour de force*, 'is the organization that I control and with which I shall outbluff the Western Allies. How? you ask.'

He answered his own question with a little metaphor he remembered from his days as a law student in Berlin. The professor of jurisprudence had used it to explain the correct approach to any problem. 'There was once a farmer, gentlemen, who wanted all his apples carefully examined for rot. So he told his labourer to grade the apples into large and small ones to put into separate boxes. That way he ensured that the apples were properly examined, though the labourer thought he was grading them. In other words the real purpose of the exercise was not the obvious one. Now, gentlemen, my plan is based on that method. I want to make the enemy believe I am doing one thing, while in reality I am doing something else. For my mission I have selected a young officer of the Armed SS, who has shown considerable bravery on the battlefield and who, in addition, speaks fluent English. He was brought up in that country. Presently he is training with the Hunting Commando. Incidentally his name is Wolf — an apt name in my opinion, for it will be his efforts which will lure our particular pigeon into the Valley of the Wolf, from which he will never return. He will be sent to England under various circumstances which I don't need to go into here, with the official mission of finding out from which part of the British coast the Invasion will sail. As you all know this would tell us where they should land in France.'

There was a mumble of agreement.

'However, that is only the mission as our man Wolf sees it. The farmer, if I may recall my image, has told him to sort the apples. That is the obvious purpose. What is his real one?'

He paused and let his words sink in.

'His real purpose is to be captured by the British at the home of one of our agents over there to which we will direct him as the means of relaying his vital discovery to us. The agent in question has betrayed us and has no means of getting out the information Wolf will bring him. The result we anticipate is that Wolf, by now exhausted and utterly confused, will reveal the second reason for his mission to England — we will drum it into his head when the time comes for his briefing — namely that we need the information in order to allow us to position a new secret mobile V-1 regiment.'

'But there is no such thing!' Rommel said.

'Agreed. But Wolf thinks there is and when the British come to hear of it, they will too. We have prepared a careful cover plan to convince them of it, independently of Wolf. Now, gentlemen, the information that a V-1 regiment could be in a position to bring a murderous fire on to the beaches where the invaders will land would definitely change the thinking of the gentlemen at Southwick House — very drastically. Not for very long, perhaps, but if this new threat were revealed to them, say in the first week of May, it could have the effect of making them postpone the Invasion till June and then it wouldn't matter any more.'

Rommel broke the silence that followed. 'A very ingenious plan, Schellenberg,' he said. 'And I think, for one, that it will work. They took the whole weight of their bombing away from targets in the Reich last autumn when they discovered the first V-1 sites.

I think that illustrates just how much they fear the missiles. Imagine what the reaction would be if, days before the invasion, they suddenly discovered that we had a whole mobile regiment of the things waiting for them? They would have to stop their men until they found out the truth of the matter and they would only have a handful of days in which to do so before the May weather broke again.'

'Exactly,' Speidel agreed.

After that the lecture dissipated into a discussion about the glorious possibilities that Operation Cuckoo's Egg opened up for them, marred only by Bittrich's sudden question, 'But if the Tommies know that this agent in England cannot pass the information Wolf brings him back to Germany and you knew in advance he couldn't...' He paused, as if he were having difficulty in formulating the remainder of his question.

'Yes?' Schellenberg encouraged him. He had been expecting the question sooner or later.

'Well, won't they begin to suspect your plan? Wouldn't they ask Wolf what was the use of the whole mission?'

Schellenberg smiled. 'An excellent question, General. But we know our Wolf. Once he discovers that there is no purpose to his mission, he will run; his history shows him to have always been a lone wolf, if you'll forgive the pun. He'll run away again.'

'And when he stops running?' Bittrich persisted. 'After all there is no way off the Island for him, and they'll have him again for their interrogations.'

'My dear General,' Schellenberg said carefully, 'when Captain Wolf stops running, he will be dead.'

That had been in January. Now this fine May morning, marred only by the smoke left from the previous night's raid, Schellenberg, sitting at his desk, reading yesterday's *Daily Mirror*, flown in specially from Lisbon, following the English of the little notice with difficulty. He could see that Wolf was still running and running. It was working.

Then he dismissed *Haupsturmführer* Wolf from his thoughts and got on with the business of running a war in which he had not believed for two years now.

BOOK FIVE: *THE BETRAYAL — YORKSHIRE (JUNE, 1944)*

'Six days to go'

CHAPTER 1

Wolf heard the Priest creep out of the room, where he sat slumped in a chair, head on his chest, eyes closed with exhaustion. He heard him go down the hall on tiptoes and pick up the 'phone. He heard the click and the few whispered, frightened words. He was not asleep. But he did not open his eyes or do anything, even when he caught the word 'police'. He was unable to force his body to move, sapped of energy by the absolute purposelessness of his mission to England.

The Priest sobbed when the police came to arrest him. 'I'm a coward,' he cried and wrung his hands like a character in a second-class film. 'I had to do it, my son. I didn't want to die.'

The middle-aged policemen, all of them wearing the faded ribbons of another war, were kind to him, muttering little words of encouragement and telling him he'd 'made a good try', as if he had been involved in some sort of sporting event instead of what he had thought was a vital mission for Germany.

About three, a very old one with white hair and an enormous belly, which bulged over his uniform trousers brought him a mug of tea, saying, 'There you are, lad, get a nice hot cup of tea inside yer. Then yer'll feel a lot better, mark my words.' At six, the same man returned with his supper — a cup of cocoa and two thick slices of bread, smeared with something white.

'Now what's this here?' he had said in surprise at the untouched cup of cold tea. 'Yer can't go on like that, lad. You've got to have something to eat and drink, yer know. Hard enough to get a little bit to keep body and soul together as it is.' He laughed heartily so that his belly trembled. 'Course,

I do my best. As you can see.' He picked up a slice of bread and proffered it to the silent prisoner. 'Now, have a try of that, son. It's best bacon dripping with a bit of onion mixed in with it.'

Almost unthinkingly Wolf opened his mouth and took the bread. And then suddenly he forgot his depression — the shock of the whole business at the Priest's vanished and he was eating the bread while the fat policeman looked down at him approvingly.

When he had gone, Wolf washed down the rest of the bread with cocoa. Suddenly he was filled with renewed hope. There was a way out! There was still hope. He wouldn't have to spend the rest of his life in some English prison, for he knew that they would blame him entirely for the Ledig business. And above all, he might be able to get back to Germany one day and answer for himself that great, overwhelming question, 'Why?'

But he knew he had to move fast. Once they had him back in London, he was finished. He'd never get out of there. His mind made up, he rose to his feet and examined the little cell.

It was about three metres square, its walls tiled a dirty mustard in the Victorian fashion. High above his head there was a small barred window, covered now by blackout shutters. He stood on the hard bunk and tested them. That wasn't the way out. They were firmly embedded in the concrete. It would take weeks to lever out those bars, even if he had something to lever them out with.

He dropped despondently on his bunk. There was nothing else in the cell, save the smelly enamel night bucket, covered with a wooden lid. Suddenly he had an idea. He got to his feet and stared at the door. Although it was constructed of massive oak boards, nailed with great iron bolts, the boards were fastened together by tongues of softer wood. He took the spoon, which was still in the mug, and poked it experimentally at one of the wedges. The wood gave a little. He did the same with the oak plank next to it. The wood did not give. Wolf ran his eye down the centre plank. There was no cross-piece at the bottom binding all the planks together. If he could free one of the planks down both sides there seemed nothing to stop him taking it out — unless there was a cross-piece on the other side of the door. He turned his body to the side and tried to judge whether he could fit through the width of one removed plank. It looked very tight, but he might manage to get through. But first of all, how was he to remove the double linings of soft wood?

He looked at the spoon. It would take him hours to grind its handle down into anything sharp enough for the job. There must be something he could use? Then he had it.

With the aid of the spoon, he began to unscrew the steel heel-plate from his right boot, bought on the Camp's black market. Whoever had possessed the boots before he purchased them had worn the curved steel plate down to such an extent that its outer edge was almost as sharp as a razor.

He began to work on the door. An hour passed. His pace had slackened now, but the floor around his feet was littered with tiny pieces of wood and there was a definite breeze of colder air from the corridor. At midnight, just after the bobby on duty had come down the corridor and opened the Judas Hole to see a sleeping Wolf huddled beneath the grey blankets — the heel-plate snapped in two. He cursed and unfastened the second plate.

By three he had cleared one whole side of the stout oak plank and about a third of the other. If there were another check now, he knew the damage he had inflicted on the door would be spotted at once. But he relied on the fact that the policemen were all old. He worked on, his fingernails bleeding. At half past three when he had about one third of the second lining to go, his final heel plate snapped.

He controlled his rage and began to look around for something to replace it. At first there seemed nothing. Then he found a long sliver of sharp enamel on the inside of the night bucket. He finally freed it, his hands lacerated and stinking so much so that he could hardly prevent himself from retching.

At four he had done it. He dropped the sliver of enamel onto the cell floor and tried the plank. It did not give. He applied more pressure like an incompetent dentist wondering if he would ever get a deeply imbedded molar out. The board squeaked in protest. Dust poured out of the cracks — the dust of a century of minor misery which the cell must have seen. He put his full weight at it. It must give now. He just caught it before it struck the flagged corridor outside. Gingerly, he lowered it noiselessly to the floor and waited.

Nothing happened. Somewhere outside in the charge room, the fat, middle-aged bobbies still slept, knowing that a war-weary Swindon went to bed promptly at ten after the pubs had closed. Nothing ever happened in Swindon on a week-day night.

Wolf turned to his side and taking a deep breath began to squeeze his way through the opening. He got through all right. Cautiously he made his way down the dimly-lit corridor, until he reached the barred gate. To his right there was a strong light where the bobbies had turned up their gas jets — he could hear the steady hiss. He could also hear the soft, controlled breathing of sleeping men. He knew that he hadn't a chance in hell of getting through the barred gate, and for a moment he toyed with the idea of attracting one of the bobbies to his cell and forcing him to give him the keys — the man could be easily overpowered. But there were always the others outside. He wouldn't be able to overpower them before they had given the alarm. No, that was not the way. He looked at his watch. He had about one and a half hours before they would wake.

Then he remembered the instructor at the Hunting Commando Lodge — a big, dark-haired Pole with a broken nose and huge paws, from which the fingernails had been removed. In his funny broken German (he was Ethnic German, but he still couldn't speak the language correctly), he had said, 'All the time when people are locked up, they think to get out — go straight in front or down. But no, down and front are always best protected. Up,' he had pointed a finger like a sausage into the air, 'Up, it is better!'

As silently as he had come, Wolf went back along the corridor, staring carefully at the dirty, flaking ceiling. Then he spotted something. Above his head there was a wooden trap. But how was he to get at it? Even when he stretched himself to his full height and extended his arms, he was still a good metre and a half away from it. He wouldn't be able to get his bunk through the gap in the door, nor even the bucket. There was nothing in the cell he could use.

Time was running out. Then his gaze fell on the gas jets. There were four of them in all, set in pairs at about two metres from each other, linked by cross pipes to a central pipe which ran down the length of the corridor's centre. For some reason — possibly because they would be easier to get at and repair that way — the cross pipes were not attached to the ceiling itself but were fixed some eighty centimetres below it — and the second cross pipe was positioned exactly below the trap!

Wolf saw the possibility at once. The frail-looking pipe might just bear his weight if he didn't stay there too long. But first of all he had to get on it. Swiftly he took off his boots and, using the laces, knotted them together and hung them round his neck. In his stocking feet, he backed off down the corridor to its furthest extent. He breathed in deeply and crouched in the position of a professional sprinter, head up, eyes staring at the dim outline of the cross pipe.

He ran forward on his stocking feet and jumped. His bloody fingers touched and held on to the narrow metal pipe. Then with all his strength he punched the square wood above his head. It gave at once and a thick cloud of dust descended on his upturned face. Eyes dilated, every muscle screaming in protest, he raised himself on the pipe and, butting his head against the trap to move it out of the way, thrust himself through the hole into the darkness of the loft. He gave himself a minute to catch his breath, sprawled full-length on the floor made of plaster and wooden laths. Then he began to crawl forward through the dusty darkness on his hands and knees, feeling every inch of the way towards some kind of skylight which he could make out far off. It seemed to take him an age to reach the light. He tried to force it. It didn't budge. Now he felt he was sufficiently far away from the sleeping bobbies to take more drastic measures. He unslung his boots from around his neck and took off his battledress blouse. He wrapped the boots in the thick khaki serge to fashion a clumsy bludgeon. Without the slightest hesitation, face turned to one side to avoid the breaking glass, he swung it against the skylight. It cracked with a noise that sounded to him as loud and as frightening as a whole battery of 'Stalin Organs' opening up. But down below there was no movement. The bobbies slept on.

Swiftly he cleared away the rest of the broken glass and crawled through the skylight onto the sloping slate roof, boots around his neck once more.

He crawled along the steep roof, slithering a couple of times and nearly disappearing over the twenty metre drop. There was no sound now, save that of his own harsh breathing and the clatter of the steam engines at the shunting yards a hundred or so metres away.

He came to the edge of the roof, and stretched himself flat near the guttering, full of bird droppings and old leaves. Carefully he peered over the side and stared down at the street below. The street was empty. He breathed a sigh of relief. He inched his way along the edge until he found what he sought: the drain pipe which led to the ground in the typically English style of outside drainage. He was just about to grab it and test it for strength, when he heard a slight cough down below. There was someone there! His eyes flashed to the right and caught the faint glimmer of a cigarette. There was someone smoking in the doorway to his right, just opposite what would be the main entrance to Swindon Police Station. Wolf knew it must be a sentry and that he must get by him if he wanted to escape. For what seemed an age, Wolf lay there in the gutter. After all this, he was going to be frustrated at the last minute! How was he going to clamber down the drain pipe without the Tommy sentry hearing him? Over at the station, a faint pink glare lit up the blacked out horizon as the trains clattered through the night, bearing their freights of death and impending destruction. What was he going to do?

Then it recurred to him that the trains passed at regular intervals, perhaps every ten minutes. When one did, the noise he would make would be drowned. He waited until the next train came. A shrill whistle broke the night. Wolf did not hesitate. As the noise of the train swelled in volume he swung himself over the side and began clambering down the drainpipe, dropping the last three metres just in time, before silence descended again on the town.

He crouched there in the darkness, watching the doorway, feeling all his human instincts swallowed by a pure animal rage at the obstacle which barred his way. But he must get by him!

He took a deep breath and started to straighten up as the mournful howl of another train's whistle signalled that it would soon provide him with the noise he needed. Wolf sprang forward, his battered hands reaching for the other man's throat.

Private Goad of the 1st Dorsets, a deserter from one of the assault divisions three days before, broke, hungry, hopeless, waiting for dawn so that he could give himself up at the police station, reacted as he had been taught these last two years. He tried to break the hold with an inner upwards sweep of his own. But his assailant was ready. He clutched his elbows together and stopped the move. Goad stared at the white blur of a face before him. He felt his strength begin to ebb. Bright red stars were exploding in front of his eyes. There was a black ringing in his ears. *He must get free!*

Frantically his fingers fumbled for the jackknife hanging at his belt — part of his D-Day equipment. With a flick of his middle fingernail he opened the biggest blade. All was beginning to go black now. He couldn't last another minute. He thrust the knife into his unknown attacker's side as they swayed back and forth in the darkness. The man grunted, but still he did not relinquish the terrible pressure. With the last of his strength, Goad thrust home his knife again and then blackness swamped him and he went limp in his assailant's hands.

Wolf did not let go. He forced his fingers to bite even deeper into the soldier's throat, afraid that one last, dying cry might betray him after all. Then, very slowly, he began to relax his hold. Nothing happened. There was no cry. Not the slightest movement.

Gently, almost reverently, he lowered the dead young man's body to the cobbles.

Private Goad, who had run away to avoid dying on an Invasion beach, had died at the hands of a German after all.

CHAPTER 2

Taylor stared down at the dead soldier in the alley. By the light of the policeman's torch he could make out the bulging eyes and the purple tongue hanging out of the wide-open mouth. 'Strangled him, he did,' the bobby said in an awed voice, 'And I thought he was such a nice lad. But he was really a cold-blooded thug like all them Jerries.'

Taylor looked at the red and black TT patch of the 50th Northumbrian Division on the dead youth's shoulder and asked, 'How did he come to be here at this time of the night?'

The bobby clicked off his torch. 'He was on the run, sir, did a bunk from his battalion, according to his adjutant, just as they were going into the — well, you know, sir,' he added.

'Invasion troops?'

'Right, sir. You know how them young lads is when they're going into action for the first time. I don't doubt we was just the same in the last lot, sir.'

Taylor nodded. In the 'last lot', they had put sandbags over the heads of such men after a frontline court-martial, tied them to a chair with their backs to the firing squad and blasted them into extinction. But he didn't tell the old bobby that; the man was too upset as it was.

'He had been inside, sir,' the policeman said, when the Squadron Leader and his two companions did not speak.

'Inside?' Gaines queried.

The bobby shook his head. 'No, sir, not that. In Swindon, we always say inside for anybody who's worked for the Swindon Railway Works. Perhaps he thought he could dodge the column back in the Works. But they wanted to see his papers and he hadn't none and so there he was with no money and nothing to eat.'

'So you think he was just wandering around, plucking up the nerve to surrender himself to the authorities when he bumped into the escaped man?' Taylor asked.

'That's about it, sir. Reckon he'd have been better off with his Battalion, taking his chance like the rest of them poor buggers.'

'There's some blood over here, sir,' the Special Branch Sergeant said, following the trail left by the escaping Wolf with his pencil flashlight.

Taylor walked over to him and spotted the line of dark dots on the cobbles. 'The deserter must have banged him one.' The Detective-Sergeant bent down and stared at the drops of blood before dipping his finger in one of them to check how wet it was.

'Still pretty damp,' he said.

'And what's that supposed to mean?' Taylor asked.

'Well, it must have happened over an hour or so ago, sir, according to PC Jones. So if the blood hasn't dried out by now, we can conclude the bugger got a nasty stab.'

'I see,' Taylor said.

The fat sergeant at the charge desk had finished making the tea for them. He thrust three chipped mugs across the desk towards them, his hands still shaking a little from the shock of the escape and the discovery of the murdered man. Nothing like this had ever happened at Swindon since the troubles in the General Strike of 1926. 'Real old sergeant-major's tea, gentlemen,' he said with fake heartiness.

Taylor thanked him with an equally fake smile.

For a moment or two they sipped the hot tea. Then Gaines said, 'He hasn't got a chance in hell, has he? No money, no food, dressed in British uniform — and perhaps, if we're to believe you, sergeant, wounded on top of it.'

Taylor nodded. 'Right. You know, after the war, we and the Yanks'll probably portray him and his kind as tough, ruthless, purposeful young thugs. I know we did after the last war. But he isn't that kind at all. He is just a scared young man running for his life.'

'He killed a man though,' the Sergeant grunted, omitting the 'sir' deliberately.

'I don't know about that,' Gaines said. He hadn't much time for introspection at the best of times, especially not at seven o'clock in the morning in some godforsaken place like Swindon. 'We'll be lucky if we survive the war, Taylor. What I'm concerned with is — what now?'

'What now?' Taylor echoed his query. 'Now we've got to find him. But there is one more thing I've got to check.'

'May I ask what it is?' Gaines said a little warily, remembering the business with the telephone the previous evening.

Taylor shook his head. 'No,' he said bluntly, putting down his mug. 'You may not. Now come on, get your fingers out, the two of you. We'd better get a shave and wash and get on after him before he does any more damage.'

Wolf, crouched behind the big pile of sleepers at the exit to the shunting yard, where the lines joined those of the goods yard, gingerly freed the bloody shirt from his side. There was a hole in his left wrist, just below the artery, which was still bleeding steadily. He twisted his body a little until he could see the wound in his side. It was not very wide and had stopped bleeding, but somehow he knew it was very deep. Each time he breathed, he experienced that deep burn of internal pain he remembered from his *Bauchschuss* outside Kiev in 1941. He told himself not to be afraid, even if the knife had punctured one of his lungs; once he got *there*, she would take care of it somehow.

He pulled the tail of his shirt round and, wincing at the pain caused by the effort of flexing his muscles, ripped it off. With part of it, he made a clumsy bandage for his wrist, pulling it very tight to stop the bleeding. Then he unbuttoned his flies and urinated on the rest of the cloth, as a form of antiseptic. He pressed the urine-soaked wad of cloth into the hole, jammed it there tightly. It hurt like hell, but he knew it was better than nothing.

Ten minutes later he heard the slow chug-chug of the goods train he had been waiting for — the one going north. He raised himself and peered over the top of the sleepers. The train was definitely taking the track north. How far it was going didn't matter. All that was important was that it was going north and it would get him out of Swindon.

He ducked hastily. The train was almost upon him now. The rattle became a roar. He caught a fleeting glimpse of the driver and his mate, black outlines against the fiery glare of the open furnace door, shrouded by the white mass of the steam. He hurtled forward. The goods was going much faster than he had anticipated. He clutched upwards desperately. His hand connected with metal. He held on with all his strength. Next instant he was swung off his feet. He clutched hold with his other hand. For a moment he was towed by the train, his boots dragged through the gravel of the track. Then he pulled himself upwards, burying under the loose tarpaulin into the soft comfort of what seemed to be empty sacks. He breathed out hard. A delicious feeling of triumph overcame him. He forgot his thudding heart, his broken hands, the deep pain. All he was conscious of was the smell of life, the knowledge that he had done it. He was free again, moving north at a steady twenty miles an hour. Happy as he had not been for many a year, he fell into an exhausted sleep.

How long he had been asleep he did not know. But now he could definitely feel a change in the train's rhythm; it was slowing down. His exhilaration had vanished, replaced by cold calculation. He must get off the train before it stopped and he knew instinctively that it was going to stop soon. He crawled out of his hiding place and lowered himself to the couplings. He had been right. Ahead of him was the sprawl of an approaching town. Every hundred metres or so telegraph poles whizzed past. He let go of his handholes and told himself he must remain loose when he hit the ground. He counted to three. Then he jumped. His feet hit the ground in two giant strides. He lost his balance. An instant later he was rolling head over heels down a sharp granite-chip embankment, coming to rest in a gasping heap at its bottom, feeling the terrible stab of pain in his side.

But there was no time to think about that now. He crouched low while the guard's van passed, then struggled to his feet and began to walk along the tracks, hoping to find a spur bearing north-east, where he might jump another train on the far side of the town ahead.

He soon discovered the disadvantage of walking along the railway line. The wooden sleepers were too close together for him to proceed at a normal pace. It was the same with the spaces between the sleepers — some were deep, their gravel gone, others were close to the surface, their gravel not dispersed yet. For a while he tried balancing on one line. But it was too slow and too strenuous. In the end he took to the little path on the side of the embankment, though it often took him down into the bushes and caused him to waste a lot of energy climbing back up again.

Half an hour later when he had begun to edge his way round the town, the embankment path took him down among some bushes deeper than the rest and it was here that he bumped into the railwayman — fell over him would have been a better description, for he was fast asleep, covered by what Wolf had taken to be a pile of abandoned coal sacks.

The railwayman recovered faster than Wolf, sprawled full-length on his face. 'I was just having a little nap, gaffer,' he gasped, seizing his long-handled hammer. He stopped suddenly when he saw that the man wasn't the 'gaffer', but a soldier, dressed in a dirty, stained uniform, unshaven and without a beret. He relaxed and said, 'You on the run, brother?' Wolf did not understand why the man called him 'brother', but he grasped at the chance offered him like a drowning man at a life belt. 'Yes, I'm a deserter.'

The little man winked. 'I thought as much. A lot of the lads is doing a bunk these days. They don't see why they should sacrifice their lives for them. What did they ever do for us workers, I ask you, brother?' The railwayman spat on the ground. '*Nowt!*'

Wolf nodded. His side was hurting like hell again after the fall and he was glad just to sit there, but soon he must make a move.

'Now of course, when they need us it's all Beveridge Plan and fair shares an' all that kind of pap. But we know what we was to them in the past, don't we, brother? Nine and a tanner a day I was getting in twenty-six to keep a wife and two kiddies on. Then when we pulled up a few fishplates and shifted a bit of rail to stop the trains during the General Strike, they put me inside for nine months.' He poked a dirty finger at Wolf accusingly. 'And do you know who did that to me, brother, and forced me missus and the kids into the spike?'

Wolf shook his head numbly, only half understanding the man's words, wondering at his sudden anger.

'I'll tell yer. Yer fine Mr Winston Churchill — that's who it was brother!' He spat again. 'So don't give me no old buck and backchat about we must pull together for the good of the country. Bollocks! What we workers has got to be out for is ourssen and our kind.' He tapped a small brass badge stuck to the front of his overalls. 'The union is what counts most, brother, not them…'

Wolf let the man rant on for a while; he was clearly harmless and quite uncurious about him. Obviously, the man had been sleeping when he should have been tapping the rails. Now he was quite happy to air his views about 'the toffee-nosed capitalists' as he called them, until it was time for him to go home. But Wolf did not have all that time. His mind made up, he butted into the railwayman's flow of words. 'Can you help me, mate?'

'How, brother?'

'I need some clothes. I can't keep running around like this. The Redcaps'd soon pick me up.'

The railwayman frowned. 'Clothes don't hang on trees these days, you know, brother. My old woman's always f—ing and blinding about she's got nothing to wear to the boozer of an evening and —'

'Clothes!' Wolf interrupted him. 'What about your jacket — it would just about fit me?'

'Get off,' the railwayman said indignantly, putting his hand protectively on the dirty jacket which lay on the floor next to him. 'It's my best working jacket, that 'un is.' The fraternal greeting was absent now.

'Well, where?' Wolf persisted.

'The shunters' hut,' the railwayman said, after a moment's thought. 'Just because they're in the drivers' union the sods think they're better than us — a lot of stuck-up buggers. There'll be clothes in the shunters' hut.' He picked up his hammer and jacket. With a kick he sent the sacks into their hiding place in the bushes and said, 'Come on. I'll show you where it is.'

The railwayman broke the window of the shunters' hut easily with his hammer. Later they'd blame the squaddie. He was in the clear. Together they clambered through. The hut, which smelled of unwashed clothing and oil, was empty save for a bare table, a few wooden chairs and the steel cabinets which lined its walls.

'They'll be in there, if they're anywhere,' the railwayman said and, lifting his hammer, smashed off the hasp of the first lock. He went down the line doing the same with each lock, leaving the doors swinging wide, revealing Betty Grable, showing her 'million dollar legs' in their full glory and flashing an impossible smile at her unknown admirers. It seemed to give him some pleasure to do so.

But Wolf had no eyes for the pin-ups. He picked up a smelly pair of overalls and measured them against his body. They looked as if they would fit. Ignoring the pain in his side, he slipped into them. While his attention was thus occupied, the railwayman dipped his dirty hand into the pocket of a donkey jacket and pulled out some money. Four single shillings and a sixpence. He thrust the coins quickly into his own pocket. He'd be all right for a couple of pints at the *Railwaymen's Arms* this evening.

Then Wolf saw the jacket. He pulled off his blouse, keeping his wounded side concealed from the other man and slipped it on. The jacket was too tight for him, even without the blouse. But it didn't matter. He could leave it unbuttoned. Swiftly the two of them clambered out of the window. 'What's the town?'

The railwayman was in a hurry now. He didn't want to be seen with the 'thief'. 'Cheltenham,' he answered. 'Give it a miss, it's thick with Redcaps.'

'I will,' Wolf hesitated a moment. It was the first time in his life he had ever done anything like this. Maggie had always been insistent that one 'never took nowt from nobody'. 'You couldn't let me have any money, could you?' he said, looking down at the ground. 'I've not got a penny.'

'I'm about skinned mesen,' the Railwayman lied. 'But you can have the last tanner I've got.' He fumbled in his pocket among the stolen coins and, pulling out the sixpence, handed it to Wolf with a magnanimous gesture. 'There you are, brother.'

'Thank you — *brother*,' Wolf said — and he was not being sarcastic as he used the word.

Thirty minutes later Wolf was on a slow goods train belonging to the LMS, heading for Birmingham.

CHAPTER 3

It was dawn. All around him the countryside was bleak, flat and empty. He had been going all night, guiding himself by the great khaki convoys roaring continuously southwards. All the sign posts had been moved years before at the threat of the German invasion. So he went in the opposite direction to the convoys, taking the little winding gravel country roads parallel to the main arteries. '

He was unbearably tired and his side hurt. He walked on a little while longer, but in the end he gave in to his weariness and, pushing his way through the thin hedge which bordered the country road, he scrambled under the brambles on the other side and crept into the ditch.

There he fell asleep at once. He woke once — he didn't look at the time on his wristwatch — and lay shivering and mumbling to himself with the cold. The sun still hung on the lip of the horizon, cold and pale, as if debating with itself whether it should make any further effort. The spasms of cold racked him like a fever. He wriggled his body inside the two layers of shirt and overalls and hoped the friction would create some warmth. He was hungry too, very hungry. His last meal had been the bread and dripping in the jail thirty-six hours before. His stomach ached with hunger.

But *Hauptsturmführer* Wolf had been wounded, hungry and cold many times before during these last five years. He did what he always did on such occasions, he 'ordered' himself to go back to sleep. His eyes closed and there was no sound save that of his gentle snores and the steady persistent roar of the Invasion convoys rolling south half a mile away.

He awoke to find the sun warming his face through the brambles and his nostrils assailed by the smell of cooking. 'Whatcher, mate, had enough kip?'

Wolf started up in alarm, the pain stabbing his side like a sharp knife. An old, old man was crouched at the other side of the brambles, squatting on his haunches like a miner, prodding at an old tin can, with a handle of wire, and stirring its contents with a twig. The old man grinned and showed a mouthful of brown decayed teeth, with gaps everywhere. 'Frightened yer, eh?' he asked good-humouredly.

'Who … what…?' Wolf stuttered, fighting hard to wake up.

'Cooper's the name,' the old man said. 'But blokes usually call me Lefty.' He held up the left arm of his stained, tattered raincoat, tied at the waist by string. The hand was missing. 'Caught a packet at Wipers.' He gave the can a final stir. 'I'm a gentleman of the road now.'

Wolf sat up. 'What?'

'A nomad.'

Wolf still looked puzzled.

The old man chuckled and rubbed his grizzled beard with the back of his black hand, the fingernails thick with years of accumulated dirt. 'All right, tramp to you.'

'Oh, I see.'

'And you, mate?' the old man said without looking directly at him.

'Brown's my name. I'm going north. I'm looking for work.'

Lefty laughed softly and began to pour the contents of the pot into a chipped white billy. 'Come off it son.' He nodded at Wolf's army boots. 'Yer on the run, aren't yer?' Wolf said nothing and watched the tramp. He poured the tea — for that was what he had been cooking over the little wood fire — into a cracked saucer he produced from his bundle, blew on it once and handed it to Wolf. 'There you are, mate. You can have firsters.'

Wolf didn't hesitate. He seized the saucer and drank the hot tea in one gulp, while the tramp nodded his approval. 'That's the stuff to give 'em, lad! You needed that, didn't you?'

Wolf spat a tealeaf out of his mouth and said, 'Yes, thanks. I was cold.'

'And hungry?' the old man asked.

'Yes.'

'Well, let me just have a sup o' tea and we'll see what we can do about it.'

The tramp finished his saucer of tea slowly, then, with the twig, he pushed aside the stones which supported the can. Beneath the stones there were four potatoes, their skins wrinkled and grey with ash. 'Hang on,' he said, as if Wolf might seize one of them in his hunger. 'Got to eat proper — have a bit of manners, yer know.' He took off his battered trilby to reveal a brown bald pate, fringed with long white hair, and searched inside it until he found what he wanted — two screws of greased paper containing salt and pepper and a little twist of something he announced was 'Maggie Ann'.

With his pocket knife, he cut a cross into two of the potatoes, and let the hot steam escape before he sprinkled the opening liberally with the spices and followed that with a dab of his margarine. 'There you are mate,' he said triumphantly. 'Couldn't get better grub than that in a British Restaurant, yer couldn't. Now tuck into it.'

Wolf 'tucked into it' greedily, burning both his fingers and his tongue, but feeling warmth and energy coming back into his frozen body. The tramp watched him with approval, taking his time, chuckling a little to himself as Wolf tossed the potato from one hand to the other.

'Why are you feeding me like this?' Wolf asked when they were finished and the tramp was beginning to roll cigarettes in the cigarette-rolling machine he had taken from the inside of his hat, filling the well with tobacco from crushed cigarette ends, collected in some gutter or other.

'I'd have done us an hedgehog too, if I'd have had time. I've got a nice juicy one in my swag.' He indicated the bundle at his side.

'Come on,' Wolf persisted. 'Why?'

'Well, I'm not funny,' the tramp said hesitantly. 'A lot of us nomads are, yer know.' He shrugged. 'I mean what woman would want to spread 'em for us — the way we look?'

Wolf waited.

'Well, I don't rightly know, son. When I first saw yer in the ditch, I thought you'd snuffed it, yer looked so bad. But then I could see yer was breathing, but not too good.' He tossed one of the limp, little cigarettes to Wolf and proceeded to roll his own with remarkable dexterity for a man with one hand. 'So I said to mesen — that lad needs a bit of grub under his belt to get him going again.'

Wolf pulled a twig from the dying fire and lit the little cigarette with it. It didn't draw very well, but it was blessed nicotine. 'What,' he said slowly, 'if I were to tell you I wasn't English?'

The tramp finished rolling his cigarette and lit it the same way Wolf had. 'So what?' he said. 'People is people, whatever country they come from. I've known some decent Paddies in my time on the road — but not many.'

Wolf took the plunge. 'I'm German,' he said. 'I'm an escaped prisoner-of-war.'

If the old tramp was shocked, he didn't show it. 'Oh, ay,' he said after a moment. 'I thought you didn't look too English. But then who does?'

Wolf looked at him in amazement. 'But I'm your enemy,' he said hotly.

'Yer no enemy of mine, son. I've got no enemies and ain't had none these twenty-odd years since I decided to become a gentleman-of-the-road. Even the rozzers and the masters in the Spike ain't my enemies. They're just doing their duty.' He smiled gently, 'By gum, they're worse off than me by rights. They're stuck where they are. Me, I can come and go, do as I please without no bosses telling me what they think I should do.'

Wolf looked at him curiously. Didn't the old man understand him? Was he dreaming all this? 'But don't you realize that I'm a German,' he said, 'a German officer...' He stopped suddenly as he felt the pain at his side. He pressed his hand to the wound, with a gasp.

The old man saw the tears of pain which washed Wolf's eyes. 'Yer in a bit of a bad way, aren't yer, mate? Come on, let old Lefty have a look-see.' He tossed his cigarette away and, without waiting for Wolf's permission, rolled up his shirt.

Lefty Cooper's smell was overpowering, but Wolf was in too much pain to care. Carefully the tramp pulled out the sodden cloth plug, then caught his breath involuntarily.

'What is it?' Wolf groaned.

'I don't like telling nobody nothing, son. But that wound don't look too hot to me; there's that pong too. I remember it from Mons.'

Wolf knew well what he meant by that 'pong'. It was gas gangrene. 'Listen,' he said. 'I have a friend. If I could only get to her, I'll be all right. Will you help?'

197

The tramp looked down at the young man's face, seeing again that German orderly who had drawn him through the mud inch by inch after his hand had been shot off, while British shells dropped all around them, alone with the dead in no-man's land. 'Of course I'll help yer, son.'

How he got through that long May day, Wolf did not know. Lefty somehow managed to get the two of them on what appeared to be an army truck full of Spaniards. The air was full of *'como's'*, *'tampoco's'* and *'pero si's'*.

He had a vague recollection of leaning weakly against the backdoor of a big house, while Lefty examined some strange chalk mark before knocking on the door, then a whispered conversation with a hare-lipped servant who opened it and receiving a couple of sandwiches of bread, smeared liberally with Golden Syrup.

He remembered them struggling to the Great North Road and the land girl in a strange hat, who wore a tie and had a mannish crop, driving them northwards in a cart fixed to the back of her tractor, ignoring the wolf whistles and the catcalls of the soldiers in the convoys heading south. Then he fell into a pain-wracked sleep in the warm hay.

He felt a little better when he and Lefty sneaked into the goods train at Retford which took them as far as Doncaster. By then it was dark, and Wolf's wound was causing him too much pain to continue. They would have to stop.

Lefty proved as resourceful as he had been all day. Crawling out of the stationary train, he led Wolf through the darkness to where the long lines of empty passenger trains were drawn up opposite the stark outline of Doncaster Cathedral. 'Got to find a dirty one,' he whispered, as they moved cautiously among them on the lookout for, the railway policemen who patrolled the yards at night.

'Why?'

'Cos yer more likely to be spotted there by the chars than the rozzers. Chars don't turn yer in.'

Finally Lefty found an empty train that suited him. 'Up front' he whispered. 'The heat from the engine comes out there, yer see, so that the first-class toffs get their toes warmed first. At that end, the heat lasts longer.'

'How do we get in?'

Lefty smiled at him in the darkness. 'Leave that to the magic box,' he said. He pulled off his battered trilby from which he had been producing odds and ends of gear all day and took out a square-sectioned key. He applied it to the door of the last first-class carriage and turned. It opened immediately. He pushed the door further open with his one hand and, stepping back, said a little proudly, 'Enter my humble abode, sir.'

Wolf staggered up the step and dropped into the deep plush of the well-upholstered seat with a grateful sigh of relief. It was like heaven. He closed his eyes and lay back. The tramp looked up at him, a worried frown on his ancient, leathery face. Then he said, 'All right, now listen, son. I'm off to see if I can rustle up some grub for us. Don't worry, I'll be back.' He took his chipped white billy out of his pack dropped the bundle on the floor of the carriage and closed the door.

Wolf was fast asleep again almost immediately, his mind a turmoil of girls with hare-lips and masculine-looking haircuts, chalk marks on doors which meant something to Lefty, flashing-eyed little men, their every second word to him '*pobre, pobre*'.

'Hey, wake up, mate. Yer sawing wood loud enough to wake half the West Riding!'

It was Lefty, crouched on the carriage floor over a flickering stump of candle. There was steam coming from his billy and on the piece of greaseproof paper spread in front of him there were two small piles of corned-beef sandwiches. 'Grub,' he announced.

Wolf sat up, realizing again just how hungry he was and knowing he needed the strength food would give him. 'How did you get it, Lefty?'

The tramp touched the side of his long nose knowingly and winked. 'Trust an old soldier,' he said. 'There's a draft of young soldiers standing up there on the platform waiting for the overnight from Edinburgh, complete with haversack rations. But they're not real hungry — they've been stuffing themselves in the YMCA all evening on bangers and cowboy beans. So, why shouldn't they feed an old soldier like me what lost his hand at Wipers, eh?' He winked again and pushed one pile towards Wolf.

'You mean you begged them?'

'Of course. Amazin' what yer can get away with when yer an old soldier what lost his hand at Wipers.' He poured a saucer of tea from the billy for Wolf. 'And I begged this here char too from the good lady at the canteen. Though good ladies of that class ain't so good, on the whole, as yer common workin' class folks. But what's it matter? We've got our grub. Char and wads — what more can yer ask, eh?' He took a deep bite into his corned-beef sandwich.

Wolf grinned in spite of his pain. Tea and corned-beef sandwiches. Life had become very simple indeed.

Just before dawn, Lefty nudged him. Wolf groaned.

'Sorry, matey,' the tramp said quickly. 'I forgot.'

Wolf looked at his watch. It was six. He sat up and felt by the tautness in his side that the wound had started bleeding again. 'We'd better get on our way,' he said.

'Not me, mate,' Lefty said firmly.

Wolf was a little shocked. In less than twenty-four hours he had come closer to the ragged, old tramp than he had to anyone else for years. 'What do you mean?'

'This is the end of my parish, son. The Big Smoke to where the Tykes start and then back again. Canny folk, the Tykes, they don't give much away so it's not worth my while to go no further.' He fussed around making a couple of cigarettes for them in his little machine and when they were safely lit, said, 'Son, I know it's not my business, but don't you think you ought to turn yersen in?' He shook his ancient head sadly. 'You know that side of yourn ain't so hot. If yer turned yersen in, the rozzers'd get you to a doctor straight off. They're not bad that away.'

'No,' Wolf said firmly. 'There's no way back for me now.'

The tramp didn't speak for a while. 'Yer, I suppose yer right son. There's no way back — for neither of us. But I'll see yer get off the station all right — at seven, when the railway police night shift go off and the new lot is still reading their *Daily Heralds* and drinking buckshee tea in the duty room.'

Lefty was as good as his word. He guided Wolf through the yards, as if he had been doing it all his life. Without the slightest hesitation, he found the loose railing in the six-foot-high fence, spiked at the top in the Victorian style. They pushed through and Lefty carefully replaced it. 'Never know, yer know,' he said. 'Might be coming this way agen.'

Wolf didn't doubt he would.

Together they walked the cobbled streets, now filled with skinny, little men, packets of sandwiches in one pocket, rolled up paper in the other, chattering in an accent that Wolf had not heard this many a year — about pigeons and whippets and ale, as they hurried to the war factories.

Lefty stopped in front of a big, begrimed Gothic church, which seemed to belong to another world than the factories and shabby red-brick warehouses all around it. 'Here we are, son, the parting of the ways.' He pointed to the tramlines set in the centre of the cobbled streets, which formed a little square in front of the church. 'Take any one of 'em in any direction yer fancy and they'll lead you through and out of Doncaster.'

'Thanks, Lefty,' Wolf said. 'I don't know what to say…'

'Don't,' the old tramp interrupted him with surprising firmness. 'Just look after yersen, that's all.'

With a painful grimace, Wolf proffered his right hand.

Lefty looked at his empty left sleeve and grinned.

'Right pair of sodding cripples, aren't we just,' he said and shook Wolf's hand.

'Yes, Lefty, cripples we are.'

'Loners, both of us. But remember this, son, loners always make it, because they rely on nobody but themsens. Be seeing yer.'

With that he turned, leaving Wolf standing there, and started looking for fag ends, left by the departing workmen in the dirty gutters. But he couldn't see a thing. His eyes were too full of tears.

CHAPTER 4

'I didn't want to shop him; he was a nice young lad, but he's in a bad way, sir. And in the end…' the old tramp shrugged and seemed unable to continue.

'All right, all right, Lefty, no waterworks,' the Inspector said soothingly and shoved the cup of tea closer to the tramp's one hand. 'You did the right thing. After all he is a Jerry.'

The tramp opened his mouth as if to say something. Then he seemed to think better of it. Instead he picked up the cup and took a deep drink.

Taylor spoke before Gaines had a chance. His voice was soft and encouraging in the manner he had cultivated assiduously over the last years. 'Did he say where he was going, Mr Cooper?'

'No, sir, he didn't.'

'Well, did you see what direction he took?' Taylor persisted.

'Not exactly, sir.'

'What do you mean?'

The tramp looked up at him. 'I've never done nothing like this all me life before, sir; at least not since I became a gentleman-of-the-road. I've allus thought, let everybody get on with it. If I don't worry you, don't worry me. But that lad needs help.'

'Of course, he does, Mr Cooper,' Taylor agreed, his voice at its most persuasive.

'Well, he didn't come back my way and he didn't go up or down the other two roads, so he must have taken the road past the church away from me.'

'Church Road?' the Inspector prompted.

'Maybe. All I know is I told him any one of them roads would take him out of Doncaster.'

Taylor looked at the policeman but he did not need to ask his question. The man knew what he wanted to know. 'Well, if he followed that road to the edge of Doncaster, sir, he'd be heading for Thorne and Goole, out into the East Riding.'

'But where the devil does he intend going to?' Gaines asked, irritated by the grimy police station, the awful provincial speech of the people, and Wolf's persistence in leading them such a damned dance.

'You don't have any people up here, do you, Gaines?'

'No, definitely not. Once we had a woman in Grimsby, she was burnt years ago. Perhaps he's heading for the ports? But does the bloody fool really think he can find a boat to take him off the Island. There hasn't been as much as a wood freighter sailing to Sweden from Hull these last twelve months.'

Taylor shrugged. 'Well, he's up to something or other.' He turned to the policeman. 'Do you think we could do something? He is very important, this man.'

'Troops are out of the question, sir. They're all moving south. But we can alert the Home Guard.'

Gaines groaned. 'Oh, my God, how are the mighty fallen? The ruddy Home Guard!'

He was stumbling over ploughed fields now, away from the roads leading to the Humber — and already he could smell the salt sea air on the breeze. To his right he could see the skyline of Goole. He couldn't be far away from the river now.

Flocks of great black crows rose slowly into the air as he approached. He blundered on blindly, drawn by the salt smell of the water. Over there was the East Riding. He was nearly home. As he went, he felt himself growing strangely lightheaded. He thought of Maggie. But only for a while. He could not concentrate, save on that river somewhere ahead. More than once he fell over a stone or a tuft of soggy grass. But every time he forced himself to get up again and continue.

To his right now he saw the round girders of the bridge and the winding approach road which led to it. He reached the edge of the ploughed land, his breath coming in broken sobs. He blundered through some bushes and stopped short. There was the Humber, grey, slow and sluggish at this spot, with oozing black mudbanks on both sides. In his exhaustion and pain, he somehow felt that once he were on the other side, all his problems would be solved and he would be safe.

He tried to pull himself together and think clearly. The river wasn't too broad — perhaps even in his present condition he might be able to swim it. The current was nothing. Yet, once on the other side, he would be soaked, noticeable, a figure of interest. There must be another way.

Slowly he walked towards the girder bridge. There was a lone car crawling across it in first gear. Then he saw the soldier's silhouette clearly against the skyline as he came out from the mass of girders, perhaps to check the driver's identity. He sank back into the bushes, absolutely exhausted. He must wait till darkness. Then perhaps the sentry would go.

'Well, sir,' the Home Guard Company Commander barked in a voice which showed that although he might be a lot fatter than he had been in 1918, he was not one bit less military, 'this is the drill.'

Gaines sighed but held his peace.

'We move in across the fields — at two o'clock there,' he pointed his swagger cane at the ploughed fields. 'That'll be numbers one, two and three platoons. Four platoon will come with me along the Goole road. Understood?'

'Understood,' Taylor said.

'Good. My intention is this — to drive him up against the Humber, if he's out there anywhere that is. Once we get him there, your Hun's had it. If he's wounded as you say he is, he'll never be able to cross it. Understood?'

'Understood,' Gaines and Taylor said in sarcastic union.

But Captain Jaques did not know the meaning of the word sarcasm especially now, the highpoint of his four year career with the Home Guard, when he was about to capture a 'dangerous escaped prisoner-of-war', as he had described Wolf to his white-haired soldiers during the briefing. He put his officer's whistle to his lips and blew hard.

The long line of Home Guards, rifles slung, sticks in their right hands, started to move forward as one, beating the grass and bushes in front of them systematically.

Jaques beckoned to them with his swagger cane. 'Follow me,' he ordered and opened the flap of his canvas pistol holster before he began to stride down the road which led out of Goole and across the bridge to Hull, at the head of his men.

'You never know,' he said significantly over his shoulder. 'You just don't.'

'Oh, my sainted aunt,' Gaines groaned in mock wonder and clapped his hand to his forehead, 'What the hell does he think this is — *Alamein*?'

Wolf woke with a start. It was nearly dark now and the traffic across the bridge had stopped altogether; so the noise of the men's voices carried a long way. With a groan of pain, he forced his head above the bush under which he had slept. Silhouetted against the sky, he could make out a long line of men with sticks, spread out some three metres apart; they were advancing steadily in his direction!

Sudden fear overwhelmed him for a minute. Then he calmed himself. He must get out of this. He was nearly home now. There was only the river to cross. He must move — and move quick. Crouched low, he doubled as best he could along the path at the top of the bank towards the bridge. As he ran he could see that it was empty. The sentry had gone off duty. With a bit of luck he could make it across without their spotting him. He ran to the corner, where the road made a right angle before it moved up a slight ramp onto the bridge itself.

He dropped just in time. A little camouflaged truck came round the bend and squealed to a halt just in front of the bridge. Men tumbled out of it — old men, he guessed, from the way they were panting — and took open positions at the both sides of the road. Further down the same road in the direction of Goole, he could hear the sounds of other men. They were beating the grass and bushes on both sides of the approach road. He was cut off from the bridge!

There was only one way left to him. He must swim the Humber.

The mud came up to his knees. It took him all his strength to lift first one foot out of the thick black mire, move forward a pace, feeling it sink once more into the loathsome stuff, and then repeat the process with his other foot. In spite of the evening cold, the sweat poured from him and the pain stabbed at his side. And all the while there was the overwhelming dread that the men on the bridge might see him. Metre by metre he edged his way forward, feeling his strength ebb from him.

'Maggie help me!' he whispered desperately, as if he were praying to some God, 'help me!'

Miraculously his strength did not fail him. He made it to the edge of the water, his chest heaving, his eyes unable to focus, hardly daring to believe what he saw there. Tethered to a stake and hidden among the bulrushes, there was a little rowing boat!

With fingers that felt like sausages, Wolf fumbled with the rope, listening to the hoarse shouts getting closer and closer. Using the last of his strength, he thrust the little boat forward into the current and clambered aboard, to collapse in its wet interior. Unconsciousness swept over him like a black coverlet, as the little boat, jogging up and down on the slack water, began to carry him away from his pursuers and on towards the sea.

CHAPTER 5

Wolf staggered up the steep grassy slope along the clifftop, the grass cropped close by the sheep, as it rose to the highest point on the north-east coast. The gulls were crying like lost children, hurtling over the chalk cliff on the wind which swept in from the sea. But Wolf saw none of this. He saw only the little clump of red-brick houses, shadowed by the few sparse trees, which dominated the height.

Somehow he had managed the fifty kilometres from Spurn Point where his little boat had finally come to rest before the Humber flows into the North Sea. He had stumbled on and on, through forgotten villages, lonely, long-unvisited beaches, abandoned farms, their owners evacuated long ago. North-East Yorkshire — at least its coastal area — had been given back to nature, or so it seemed. Even Bridlington, through which he had just come, appeared deserted, the tall Victorian houses along the Promenade empty, their windows broken, rusting barbed wire running for miles along the beaches where he had once played as a child. He thought he vaguely remembered a shot, a cry of alarm. But he couldn't be sure. His mind was full of Maggie.

More than once he fell, as his feet sank into some rabbit hole in the grassy down. But he no longer felt the pain. He struggled to his feet again and went on, his eyes wide and staring, on to the village, and the house from which they had dragged him, a frightened, sobbing child, so long before.

It started to rain — a thin, bitter drizzle straight from the North Sea. It streamed down his face like cold tears. His clothes were drenched within seconds; they clung to his weary body in all their miserable dampness.

Now she would be waiting for him at the kitchen door, as she had when as a boy he had come running home from the Council School. He could already see her: big, capable, greying hair tied back in a bun, long white apron — 'pinny' she called it — reaching to her calves, its surface stained where she had rubbed her flour-covered fingers against it.

He staggered past the first house in the hamlet, half-made of timber, half of 'cobbles', the thick, round white stones dragged up the cliff from the beach far below. Once it had been lived in by the 'Mad Major', a shell-shocked, crazy soldier of the First War, who had marched down the street with his stick under his arm, as if he were on parade, saluting lamp posts and letter boxes. Now it was abandoned, its windows boarded up, the shingles gone from its roof.

'She'll be there, Maggie'll be there,' he said in English, in the accent of his youth, and the howling sea-wind snatched the words from his mouth.

He stumbled on, half-running, half-walking, the blood oozing unnoticed down his side, shoulders bowed, arms swinging loosely. He saw the little grey spire of the chapel which belonged to the 'Big House', which the 'Meester' (as they had called him) had allowed the villagers to use on Sundays. Maggie's boarding house was just in front of it, hidden from view still by a row of stone cottages. He quickened his pace, swaying from side to side, the rain lashing his face, the wind buffeting his body, as if the elements themselves were trying to stop him reaching her.

From far away came the sound of a racing motor and an urgent, ringing bell. He dismissed the sounds. He was nearly there now. The sick, haunted misery of his dying face was transformed into an overwhelming look of ecstatic anticipation. He swung round the corner and skidded groggily to a stop.

Maggie's house wasn't there! Where it had once stood, there was a great hole, already long overgrown with weeds, with a notice, already fading, stuck in a mound at the side. His crazed eyes took in a couple of words: 'DANGER … SUSPECTED BOMB…' Then he could read no more.

He leaned weakly against the wall of a cottage and howled, his face raised to the sky, the rain streaming down his contorted features — '*Maggie!*'

Gaines, who heard it as the Bridlington police car squealed to a stop, never forgot that cry to his dying day. 'It was like the cry of a trapped animal. It was horrible. Even today, it still makes me shudder when I think of it.'

'Wolf.'

Slowly Wolf turned round and saw Taylor. 'Where is she?' he croaked. 'Maggie, where is she?' Taylor did not know who she was. But in their ride up to the clifftop village from Bridlington, the police had told him enough. 'One of your bombers dropped his load here. The few survivors were evacuated inland. There are still unexploded bombs on…'His words trailed away to nothing. Wolf was no longer listening. He was staring at the weed overgrown hole, his pale face overcome with grief, the tears streaming down his cheeks.

'We'd better get him to hospital,' Gaines said. 'The poor bugger's dying on his feet!'

Taylor held up his hand. 'One minute. First I must ask him something. Gaines and you two men,' he indicated the two middle-aged policemen, 'would you please leave us for a moment.'

Puzzled and unwilling, the three moved back a dozen yards or so down the village street.

'Wolf,' Taylor said gently.

Wolf looked up, his hair soaked with rain and plastered over his forehead.

'We killed her,' he said in a daze. 'We killed Maggie.'

Taylor was kind but firm. 'Wolf, I must ask you a question and then we'll get you to hospital straightaway.'

Wolf did not seem to understand. He stood there, swaying groggily, his eyes — once so grey, bold and contained — seeing nothing, the tears streaming down his face without restraint.

Taylor raised his voice. 'Did you ever see these missiles Schellenberg told you about, the mobile ones?'

Wolf looked at him blankly.

'Wolf, I'm talking to you! Your life is at stake. Answer me and I'll get you to hospital. Did you see those mobile missiles with your own eyes?' Taylor grew angry suddenly — angry at the bitter rain, the boy's silence, the whole bloody war. 'Don't you realize that they played you for a fool all along?' he shouted against the wind. 'You were a plant, expendable, cannon-fodder! They knew you could never get the information out of the country. That wasn't their intention at all. They wanted you to make us believe that they had some new missile and make us postpone the invasion.' He caught hold of himself again. 'Wolf, you're dying boy. I must get you to hospital soon.'

The words penetrated Wolf's brain with terrible slowness. *Plant ... expendable ... cannon-fodder.* So they had betrayed him from the very start. It had been to no purpose. They had betrayed him and they had killed Maggie, for he knew now that *they* had done it. 'No,' he gasped, 'I never saw them. Just a photograph, that's all.'

Taylor breathed out a sigh of relief. 'Thank God for that,' he said aloud in English. That confirmed what Winterbotham had had to say — the 50th Assault Engineers did not exist. Any fool could mock up a fake photograph of a mobile missile. 'All right, Wolf, we'll take you down to Bridlington Hospital now.' He reached out one hand to steady the German and turned his head to call up the car.

In that instant, Wolf summoned up the last of his energy. He pushed aside the hand and the next moment he was running down the wet path to the cliff edge.

'Stop!' Taylor yelled, knowing already what he was going to do.

'Stop it, you fool!' the Bridlington policeman cried. At this spot the cliff is four hundred foot high.

Wolf ran on, staggering wildly from side to side. Taylor ran after him. But the path was treacherous. His feet skidded from under him and he sprawled full length on his belly. Desperately he raised his head and yelled at the top of his voice, '*Wolf, stop!*'

But Wolf, on the edge of the cliff, the rain and the wind lashing furiously at his clothes, wrapping them tightly against his thin body, hardly hesitated. Taylor caught one last wild glimpse of his tragic face as Wolf flung up his hands like a professional high-diver and went over the edge.

CHAPTER 6

Sandys' call was waiting for him when they got back to the police station. But he was soaked to the skin from peering over the side of the cliff for a body which, unknown to him, had already been claimed by the sea for all times; so he made the Head of the V-Weapons' Committee wait until he had finished a mug of tea laced with rum.

Sandys was obviously impatient. 'My God, man, what took you?' he demanded.

'Nothing of importance,' Taylor answered tonelessly. 'The man in question committed suicide.'

Sandys dismissed the information ruthlessly. 'Did you confirm what we wanted to know? The PM's in a terrible state and you can imagine what General Eisenhower is feeling like.'

'Yes.'

'Well?'

'It was a plant,' Taylor answered. 'The German had never seen one, just a photograph, obviously a fake.'

'I see.' Sandys absorbed the information at the other end for a moment. 'You realize that the whole future course of the war could well depend upon whether we go ahead with you know what now or postpone it to a later date?'

'I do,' Taylor said slowly 'It is my considered opinion that they do not have them.'

And I suppose for those few words Squadron Leader Eric Taylor deserved to die, for with them he destroyed the basis of the plot to kill Hitler: the war would go on for nearly another year, swallowing millions more young men into its insatiable maw.

'Thank you very much, Squadron Leader,' Sandys was saying. 'We are all very grateful to you. I can assure you that your efforts will not go unnoticed. General Eisenhower himself...'

But Taylor was no longer listening. His job was finished now. The 'phone still held in his hand, he was staring blankly at the sea through the rain-soaked window. It was as empty and as desolate as his own heart.

ZERO!

They met in the library of Southwick House at 4.15 that afternoon of Sunday, 4 June to listen to the tall, gaunt Scots meteorologist. They were all there — Eisenhower, Montgomery, Ramsey, in charge of the Naval forces, Leigh-Mallory, head of Air, Tedder, Eisenhower's Deputy. Outside the wind howled through the pine trees behind the big house and the rain lashed against the windows in bitter squalls. Over the sea, the barrage balloons danced like crazy airborne elephants.

But to Stagg's professional eye, the wind was not as severe as it had been that morning and the rain was not as strong. It was beginning to stop. The front he had predicted, which would give them 5/10ths cloud, cloud-base 2,000-3,000, and reduced winds, was moving in and would ensure a fair period over the Channel till at least dawn on Tuesday.

'Well, gentlemen,' Stagg said in his soft but firm voice, knowing that these were the most important words he would speak in his whole life, 'I see no substantial change from my forecast of this morning. What change there is, is of a positive nature.' He looked away from the rain outside. 'A fair interval is setting in at Portsmouth. It'll clear all of Southern England overnight and probably last till Tuesday.'

A few questions were asked. Tedder requested him to explain what had happened to clear the warm air, which had caused all the trouble. Stagg explained that a front, which twenty-four hours or so before had turned westward into the new depression off Nova Scotia and Newfoundland, had abruptly cut away down south, swept through Ireland and was now sweeping through Southern England. Then he and his staff were ushered out into the hall to wait with the rest of the staff officers, standing around in little knots, not talking much, just waiting for *that* decision.

They didn't wait long. Montgomery, Ramsay, Leigh-Mallory, all had their final say. There was a moment's silence when they were finished. Then Eisenhower made his decision. He said, 'Okay. We'll go.'

At midday on that Tuesday, 6 June, 1944, with the Anglo-Americans pouring ashore everywhere in Normandy, Schellenberg sent off two messages in the *Abwehr* code by the Enigma coding machine. One was to Skorzeny. It read 'Operation Cuckoo's Egg failure'. The other was to Rommel at his HQ at La Roche-Guyon. It read: 'What now?'

Both were picked up and deciphered immediately by the boffins at Bletchley, but neither they nor the 'Shadow *OKW*' could make much sense of the Schellenberg messages. So they went into the secret files of the SIS where they rest to this day, probably, gathering dust and still unexplained.

On the afternoon of 17 June, 1944, Adolf Hitler arrived at the Valley of the Wolf to supervise the V-1 campaign and discuss the Allied Invasion with Rommel.

Desperately Rommel tried to convince the Führer that the end was close, while Hitler pecked at his vegetarian lunch, after the two SS men, who stood behind his chair the whole time had tasted his food in the manner of some Eastern potentate.

The air raid sirens sounded and they continued their discussions in the shelter. Rommel was nearly at the end of his tether. He told Hitler that the whole Normandy front would fall apart soon. The same would happen in Italy too and before long the Anglo-Americans would be on German territory itself. He *must* sue for peace at once!

Hitler flushed and barked at the Field Marshal, who had once been his favourite, 'Don't attempt to mix in politics, Rommel. They are nothing to do with you. Confine your efforts to the Normandy front. That's your job.'

Rommel knew then that the Army must carry out the assassination. Time was running out fast. The Führer only had one more day in France.

That night he conferred with Speidel. On the morrow Hitler would visit the Field Marshal's HQ at La Roche-Guyon. If they were going to do it, they would have to do it then. Hastily Speidel set about making preparations for the assassination.

But it wasn't to be. An errant V-1, destined for London, turned a full circle that night and landed in the compound directly above the Führer's bunker at the Valley of the Wolf. No one was hurt and not much damage was done. But it was enough for Hitler, who had sworn that very afternoon that the 'V-weapons would be decisive against Great Britain'. He ordered his car and he fled back to Metz. One hour later Speidel was ordered to cancel all plans for the Führer's visit: he was already on his way back to Berchtesgaden.

One month later, while the Imperial Guard of the Armed SS bled to death in a hopeless offensive in Normandy, Rommel was on his way back from a conference at the Battle HQ of Panzer Group West when his Mercedes was spotted by British fighters, hopping across the fields at tree-top height. Rommel shouted to his driver to race for the cover of the nearest village. The Sergeant clamped his foot down hard on the accelerator. But the fighters were already on them, the eight Browning machine guns on each plane chattering wildly.

The driver was hit in the back. He lost control of the Mercedes, slumping over the wheel. At eighty kilometres an hour, it slammed into a tree at the side of the road. Rommel flew through one of the doors and hit the road. He blacked out immediately.

Unconscious and gravely injured, with only weeks to live, he was carried to the nearest village. Its name was Ste Foy de Montgommery!

By then Squadron Leader Taylor had been dead just over four weeks. Ironically enough he was killed by one of the only three of the eighty-odd missiles fired on 17 June, to impress the Führer, which reached the London target area. He had been alerted by the sudden putt-putt of what sounded like a two-stroke motorbike and realized immediately what it was. He had run rather heavily — because he had been drinking since midday — for the shelter of a nearby railway bridge. As the ton of high explosive hit the bridge above him and the world came apart in a roar, he saw Wolf once again, as if in a dream, as he swayed at the edge of that cliff and looked back for the last time. But the face above the black jacket wasn't Wolf's. It was George's.

A NOTE TO THE READER

Dear Reader,

If you have enjoyed this novel enough to leave a review on **Amazon** and **Goodreads**, then we would be truly grateful.

Sapere Books

Sapere Books is an exciting new publisher of brilliant fiction and popular history.

To find out more about our latest releases and our monthly bargain books visit our website:
saperebooks.com